IN EARTHEN VESSELS

by

Chandler Davenport

In Earthen Vessels
by Chandler Davenport

Copyright 2002 Chandler Davenport

All Rights Reserved. No part of this publication may be reproduced, stored in a retrieval system or transmitted in any form or by any means, electronic, mechanical, photocopying, recording or otherwise, without the written permission of the author.

Cover Design: William James Brown

This story is a complete work of fiction and is not meant to portray any actual people or events. Any similarity to persons living or dead is entirely coincidental.

Cross Timbers Books (http://crosstimbersbooks.com)

ISBN: 978-1-4303-0814-0

Printed in the United States of America.

Second Edition

He was only fourteen in 1950, but he had to take on manhood early. The depression that the rest of America had clambered out of a decade earlier still hung on in rural Oklahoma. A lot of people had solved that problem, in a way, by taking to the road west, lured by the golden promise of a better land; but those who were too poor or too proud or too stubborn to leave held on. Those who were poor, proud, and stubborn, like his family, managed to build a life out of corn bread, poke greens, labor and hope. It made them a special breed. But Jody didn't know that.

Chapter One

Jody trudged out of the sandy country road into a Y-shaped gravel patch and turned right where the glistening black asphalt ribbon spilled down a gentle slope into Trasherdell. In the shimmering heat of late June, the battered houses clung around Highway 80, huddled closely together at the center of the clump where storefronts faced off against one another, gradually thinning out to the fringes where isolated houses and sheds lost themselves in timber and field. He stopped in the shade of a scraggly blackjack, wiped his face on his sleeve, and absently started counting the houses. This is where the town folks live, he thought. I don't belong here.

He kicked pebbles out of the shady spot and made them dance on the asphalt. His conscience said to get on with it, but he squatted down in the shade for a few minutes. He wanted keenly to turn around and go back. He thought of how John Mark must have felt when he left Paul and Barnabas and went home to Jerusalem. But he couldn't go home and be ashamed in front of the family, like he'd put his hand to the plow and turned back. All the same, he was scared and sick at heart.

He stood up and made himself stride out into the sunlight again. At the very edge of the settlement he hesitated only a moment, then turned up a long driveway. It was simply two worn tracks in the weeds leading to a weathered little clapboard house. A big black car sat in the middle of a dusty bare spot encircled with weeds. An ancient cedar, half of its limbs dead, gave scanty shade at the edge of the plot, and a dilapidated stuffed chair, faded colorless with sun and rain, was snubbed up against the scaly trunk. Its legs were gone and the ragged seat was flat on the ground. Under the car, an aged dog had worn himself a wallow and lay there now looking at Jody out of bloodshot eyes, his chin flat in the dirt.

"Good dog," Jody said. The dog did not move. Jody squatted down and reached out a hand. A husky, tired growl sounded in the dog's throat, and his lip barely curled to show yellowed, rotten teeth. Jody drew back his hand. They exchanged a long stare. There wasn't anything to fear from the dog. He looked as if he hadn't the strength or will to bite, as if his few carious teeth would simply break up if they closed firmly on a calloused hand. The growl itself was bluff. Clearly, though, he didn't want to be bothered. Watching those dull brown eyes, Jody realized why. The dog was dying, and wanted to get it over with.

"Better leave that dog alone, young fella," said a coarse bass voice.

A man came around the car slowly, scooting himself along backwards on his hands, dragging his legs lifelessly. Jody stood up quickly, startled. The big man scooted himself across to the old chair and hoisted his huge buttocks up into the seat.

Laboriously the dog dragged himself from under the car and stood in a painful crouch. The bones stuck out all over his body, great bare spots showed in his fur, his leathery scrotum dragged the ground. Deliberately, as if considering every movement carefully, he shuffled over to the man's side, put his chin across one sprawled leg, and lay down gingerly.

The man put his hand softly on the dog's head. He didn't pet him, though, or fondle his ears, merely let the hand lie there unmoving. He was silently looking Jody up and down. To cover his embarrassment, Jody put out an elbow and leaned casually on the fender.

"Don't sit on that car," the man said.

Jody snapped upright and looked away while his ears tingled. He strolled over and sat on the weeds at the edge of the bare spot. The man was still studying him; Jody gathered his courage and stared back. He was a big man, not tall but stout with a paunch, broad hands with stubby fingers, thick hairy arms, legs—swollen, that was it. He had a round red face and a shock of iron-gray hair, ill-trimmed.

"That dog's sick," Jody said at last.

"Yeah. He sure is." The man turned his eyes to the dog and looked him over slowly. There was a little edge of anger in his voice.

"If I was able, I'd take him somewheres away from the house so Rose couldn't see or hear, and I'd kill him. I'd borrow the marshal's gun maybe or just take a club to him. He's near dead already." He paused and shifted his hand on the dog's head. "But I can't do a damn thing. Just gotta let him tough it out."

They were quiet again. The cuss word bothered Jody. That kind of talk was never allowed at home—not that he wanted to talk like that. He wanted to get up and go, but he'd told himself he'd try at every house, and it wouldn't do not to try here, at the first place he came to. He couldn't find a way to ask, though.

"What's your name, boy? What do you want?" He said it roughly, but it was like the dog's growl.

"Jody. Jody Carpenter. I want a job. I got to make us some money."

"Carpenter," the man said. He studied Jody's face. "You're Josh Carpenter's boy, ain't you?"

Jody nodded.

"I knowed your dad. Ain't seen him in years though. He's a good man." It sounded like an apology of sorts. "Well, you sure come to a hell of a town to find a job. What kind of job?"

"Any kind. I work hard, and I work cheap." He hoped that sounded right.

"Ain't you got work enough at home? If I know your daddy, unless he's changed he'll work your young butt off."

Jody grinned. "He ain't changed. It's the drought. Everything's already burned to a crisp, no crops this year at all. Maybe if it rains late, we can plant some cowpeas. He's gone to the city hisself on the Greyhound to try to find work."

"And that's what you'll have to do too, if you want a paying job."

"I ain't old enough. They won't hire you till you're sixteen."

"Shit, tell them you're sixteen. You could pass fer sixteen."

"I ain't gonna do that," Jody said.

The man raised an eyebrow. For the first time, there was the hint of a smile. "Let's see now. You're willing to break the law, or have someone else break the law fer you, but you ain't willing to lie."

Jody flushed, but he faced the question head-on. "I reckon that's about right," he said. He could explain it, he thought, if he had to, before God at the judgment, but he wasn't going to try to make it clear to this old man. It would have been different if Preacher Whitecloud had asked, or Sister Green.

The man gave a short laugh. "I guess you're Josh's son, all right."

"If you got a hoe or a scythe," Jody said, "I could cut down some of those weeds around the house. When they get dry next month, you could have a fire and maybe burn the house down. I could fix them winder screens where they're coming apart."

"I don't deny all that needs doing, but an old crippled man, I can't pay money fer something I don't absolutely have to have. Now Rose can do things like that. She's stronger'n any man." His voice had softened, and as he spoke to Jody he began to stroke the old dog's head. After a moment he said, "Tell you what. If you'll kill this old dog fer me, I'll give you a dollar."

Jody looked into the dog's eyes. "I can't do that," he said.

"Yeah. That's what I figgered."

A tall, stocky woman pushed the door of the house open with her buttocks, carrying a cup in each hand. Over a shoulder, she said, "I got your coffee. How's my old Rex dog doing today?"

When she turned she saw Jody sitting in the weeds. "Why, Bill, I didn't know you had company. What'd you let him sit down on the ground fer?" She handed Bill one of the cups and set the other one on the running board of the big car. "I'll get you a chair, young man."

Jody scrambled to his feet. "Thank you kindly, Ma'am, but I gotta go. Please don't bother."

"This here's Jody Carpenter, Josh's boy," Bill said.

"Well of course it is. I seen you once with yer dad years ago. You was just a tyke. I'm Rose Becker, and this here's my husband Bill, which I know ain't had the good manners to interduce hisself." She took Jody's hand and pumped it hard, like a man's handshake. "Where have you got to run off to so quick on a fine morning, that you can't set a bit and have a cup of coffee?"

"I gotta find a job," Jody said.

"You go downtown," Bill said. "Ain't no point going to these folks' houses. Ain't nobody in all Trasherdell got the money to hire fer more than a odd job or two, 'cept of course Judge Hanks and maybe Doc White. What you need is a steady job. You try the grocery store and Art's Cafe."

"Hey, Bill, he ought to try the marshal. I bet the marshal needs help with the animals and the garbage."

"Likely so," Bill said, "but he's so stingy he won't pay nothing, and he's mean as hell."

"Aw, Bill, you ought not say that. The marshal's just different."

"Stingy," Bill said, "and mean."

"I'm good with animals," Jody said.

"You try the marshal," Rose said, with a nod.

He gave up his plan to knock at every door and went straight downtown. He was still scared, but some of the mystery of the task was gone now that he knew where to go. The town had been throughout his childhood a place he had seen rarely except on Christmas and the Fourth of July, when he and Tommy went with his dad to buy some treats at Newby's Grocery. Even when he started high school last year he seldom went downtown because he didn't have money to spend there like other kids. On his lunch hour he would read in the library, and when school was over he would start out immediately on his four–mile walk home. He knew who the marshal was, and the judge and Art who owned the cafe, but they were shadowy characters from another world, less familiar than the cows or even the very trees of his home.

He remembered the judge. It must have been five years back. He and Tommy had been standing in the store looking at the candy in the glass case while their dad waited to pay for the flour and salt and coal oil. There was this heavy, balding man in a white shirt who said right out to their dad, "Hey, Josh, I need to buy me some of that candy corn. Do you care if these boys help me eat it?"

His dad had looked kind of funny but then grinned and said, "Sure, Judge, they're much obliged."

The judge bought a pound of candy and sat with the boys on the porch of the store while the three of them ate most of it. His dad had taken a long time to load their stuff in the wagon. The judge had wanted to know how to tell a horse's age from his teeth (and him an educated man, and not know that), so Jody had explained it to him. Then it was time to go home, and the judge gave him the rest of the candy, sack and all. He said he had all he wanted of it, and why not take the rest to his mama since it was Christmas.

On the way home, his dad had said, "That was Judge Joe Hanks. I wouldn't let just anybody do that."

He decided he would rather work for the judge than for the marshal. He knew the big white house a block from the highway belonged to the judge. It was conspicuous even from the schoolyard, since it was the only two-story house in town. He approached it with his heart thumping. It gleamed in the morning sun like a church. The picket fence was freshly painted and climbing rose ran over the lattice on the porch. The judge himself was sitting on the porch alone, dozing in a white canvas chair with a book laid open upside down on his paunch. Jody opened the gate softly and made himself walk boldly up to the porch railing, where he stood waiting for the judge to open his eyes.

While he waited, he got his speech ready. He'd say, "Morning, Judge Hanks, I'm Jody Carpenter. You bought me some candy corn once. I wonder maybe if you need a real good handy man." As he looked around the house and yard though, there didn't seem much to do. The lawn was trimmed, the porch was swept clean, even the brass knocker shone. Why should the judge hire him anyway? Obviously the judge had all the help he needed. All Jody's resolution began to leave him. The judge hadn't stirred. Slowly, quietly, Jody backed away from the porch, eased himself out the gate, and walked quickly away.

In the end, he went to work at the Marshal's Animal Store. He would rather have worked at Art's Cafe or Newby's Grocery. But he was only a thin, awkward kid with pimples, with no clothes but his work clothes; besides, he was shy. Of course he couldn't get a job like that. But for what the marshal needed, he was just the man.

The work was hard, dirty, unpleasant, but most of all, the marshal was a hard man to work for. Try as he might, Jody couldn't like the man. The best thing about the job was that he got to go home every weekend. Every Saturday he would come home late, get his belly really full for the first time in a week, and then get a real bath in the galvanized wash tub. Afterwards his mother would wash his few clothes so she wouldn't have to wash on the Lord's day. About sunset his dad would come trudging up the road, bone-tired after his long walk from where the Greyhound had let him off, but whistling or singing to himself. Then Tommy would play the guitar and they would sing, and finally the whole family would sit up talking until they couldn't stay awake. On Sunday after church, Jody ate all he could hold. Then he put his clothes in a sack and walked the four miles back to town. Through the week, he ate and slept at the marshal's house. That was part of his pay.

The marshal was the entire police force of Trasherdell. He was also the dogcatcher, the sanitation department, and the sole dispenser of hunting and fishing licenses. None of his duties took much of his time. Maybe it wasn't true that nobody in Trasherdell broke the law, but there hadn't been a violent crime in living memory, and the marshal hadn't arrested anyone in years. About all his marshaling amounted to was that he wore a gun in a holster and a badge. Each morning he strapped on his holster, and each evening he took it off, but (unless it was Sunday) left the badge pinned to the same sweaty shirt he would pull on again the next morning. After his first pot of coffee, he would climb into his old Ford pickup and rattle off to collect the garbage and trash in four green oil drums wired loosely in the pickup bed. Whoever wanted a license had to hang around the store until the marshal came back. Then for two dollars the marshal would supply a greasy piece of paper, laboriously written out in indelible pencil, smudged with his thumbprint where he tore it from the rumpled pad.

There wasn't much pay in all that, and little reason Trasherdell would ever pay him more. So some years ago the marshal had taken advantage of his various roles and opened the Animal Store. The store was a natural extension of his role as dogcatcher. He had leased an old filling station that had gone broke, built some chicken–wire cages in the garage and grease pit, and strung hog wire around a quarter–acre of the large weedy field in back. Into this pen he dragged some rickety outbuildings that had stood unused and unnoticed on the old Jamison place. Nobody had lived there since Jamison died a decade ago because the estate was tied up in a lawsuit between Jamison's daughters. Since the daughters never came to Trasherdell and never would come, they wouldn't know whether the outbuildings were there or not. From the streets of the town, from up and down Highway 80 and from the surrounding countryside, the marshal scavenged animals: dogs, cats, rabbits, squirrels, turtles, owls, assorted wild birds, even stray chickens and guinea hens. Anyone coming to claim any of this stock could do so, after minimal proof of ownership, by paying a fine and costs; whatever went unclaimed was for sale.

Jody's main job was to care for the animals. He fed the dogs and the more exotic animals, scooped out their pens, dusted them for fleas, and now and then buried a carcass in the huge weed–grown lot behind the store. He also helped the marshal on his garbage run, swept the store, made coffee and ran odd errands. Whenever he could, he haunted the office, where he could listen to the loafers talk. The front of the store became as near a town hall as Trasherdell ever had. It was the police station, license bureau, sanitation department and animal shelter all jumbled into one grimy desk. There was a pop box, a wood stove, and some battered chairs and crates where the marshal's friends came to smoke and loaf and spit their snuff and chewing tobacco toward an old zinc bucket. The ministers of the town's three churches avoided the place on principle because there was a lot of loud and vulgar talk there. Most other men of the town at leisure to do so would turn up at the marshal's from time to time, and Doc White and Judge Hanks were regulars. The marshal was a moody host, but he seemed to enjoy having everyone around him. He kept a coffeepot available at all hours.

The marshal kept a small stock of stale dog food and cat food, but the pets who stayed in the Animal Store didn't eat any such fancy fare. What they ate depended altogether on what the three hundred citizens of Trasherdell put in their garbage on any given day. Jody would jump out of the Ford, gingerly sort the garbage, and divide it into four categories: inedible (worthless), inedible (salable), food (spoiled beyond use), and food (good enough for the animals). Whatever was thrown into the fourth drum, Jody would sort carefully and portion out to the inmates as sensibly as possible. Animals, sufficiently hungry, would eat a surprising range of stuff, he discovered; nevertheless, the mortality rate at the Animal Store was pretty high. Jody soon became an experienced mortician.

Ever so often a dog would burrow and tear his way out of his pen and wreak what carnage he could on the smaller inmates before he escaped the Animal Store and Trasherdell forever.

It might look like a shaky business, but measured in terms of the economy of Trasherdell the marshal did pretty well. There was not much income from sale of his meager stock of feed, leashes, collars, and ornaments. He didn't sell very many animals to the townsfolk, either; he made more from fees and costs. Sometimes he and his skinny wife made a meal from a chicken. He managed to sell some pups, kittens, birds, and wild animals in the city, though. He would run a small ad in the city paper, offering to bring several specimens to a prospective buyer's home for convenience, and more often than seemed likely someone would write in response. On these occasions he would put on a tie, scrub the puppies and brush the kittens he picked to show, and take some birds or a possum in a cage, and usually manage a sale or two at an exorbitant price, if the clients were inexperienced and gullible.

He had another game too that worked very well when it worked at all. He offered to board dogs at the "well–known Trasherdell Kennels." As a convenience to the client, he would come pick up the animal and deliver it again on the appointed day. If a client asked to see the kennels, the Marshal would say he was full up at the moment but would call back when he had room. When luck was with him, he would get a docile, healthy animal who could be fed sparingly for a while, then grudgingly fattened and sleeked before the time to be returned. In the meanwhile, for compensation, a male dog might be put to stud for the half dozen woebegone bitches the marshal kept for breeding.

All the animals were gaunt and ill kept, but the breed bitches were piteous, Jody thought. Their ribs showed through their skins like the slats of a corn crib and their backbones stuck up like dead tree limbs sunk in the sand of the creek. Their huge dugs hung to the ground and swayed and flapped when they walked. They all cared lovingly, ferociously for their pups, as though they really knew and resented the unlikely future of whatever was born at the Animal Store.

As soon as the pups could be weaned, the marshal began watching for signs that a bitch was in heat, so she could be bred again.

The marshal didn't like animals, and the feeling was mutual. The bitches especially would bare their teeth and snarl at him quietly, their bodies curled round their pups. At such times the marshal might ignore them, or he might take down a club he had made by stitching together four thicknesses of harness leather and administer a ritual beating. Afterward the culprit bitch would slaver and whine softly for a while, crawl gently around her pen, and cower at his appearance, but she didn't seem to like the marshal any better.

On one such occasion, after the beating had gone on for a dozen strokes, Jody ventured a protest. The snarls that had punctuated the first lashes had gradually become only howls of pain. "Hey," he said to the marshal, "don't you think that's enough?" But his voice came out shaky and not very loud.

The marshal looked at him for a minute, the leather club hanging from his right hand and his left hand holding the collar and muzzle of the wailing bitch; he seemed to be thoughtfully considering whether he should beat Jody instead. When the punishment was resumed, Jody slunk off, amid the loud howls. Meanwhile the whole population of the Animal Store joined the bitch in an uproar, a chorus of barkings, flutterings, and shrieks. As usual, it lasted for a quarter-hour after the marshal hung up his club.

If only he were a grown man, Jody thought more than once. He didn't see much he could do about the marshal, but he made what compensation he could to the animals. He got along well with them, and the marshal was willing enough to let him assume all responsibility for their care. He fed them as best he could, kept the pens cleaner than they had ever been, sat up with the bitches when it was time for them to whelp, cleaned up after them, and dutifully dragged away the dead for burial.

The first time a bitch had a litter, Jody stayed at the store all night to watch and to help. That was when he decided he would rather sleep at the store than at the marshal's house. The store smelled terrible until he got used to it, but it was friendlier there among the animals. Besides, he didn't like being watched by the marshal and his hungry-looking wife while he ate. He told the marshal, if he'd just bring him something to eat each day in a paper sack, he'd stay at the store to care for the animals. The marshal said that was fine with him. He didn't bring Jody much to eat, though.

When a bitch came into heat, the marshal would move her to a small run and shelter away from the rest of the pens, kept only for this purpose. Then he would bring to her whatever he had on hand in way of a dog, hound or terrier or mutt, it didn't matter. Certainly he would use whatever healthy, well-kept specimen he might be boarding at the time that might get him some good pups to sell. The marshal would squat on his haunches, chewing his tobacco methodically as the dogs performed their crude courtship, watching without comment and with little apparent interest. Jody would watch too, trying to appear as uninterested as the marshal but in truth fascinated and aroused.

About the third time they took a bitch to the run, the marshal left to get himself a Coke from the pop box. He returned to find Jody on all fours, watching with fascination as the dogs coupled. The boy blushed red all over, but the marshal just laughed shortly and said, "Well, boy, you seem to get so much fun out of this I'm gonna let you supervise it from now on." Then he spat, tongued his tobacco in a wad into his cheek, and took a long haul from his Coke as though nothing had happened. After that time, when a bitch was ready, the marshal would say, "Take Junie to the run and bring her that liver pointer we're keeping." Jody would do the rest.

The incident left him shaken, ashamed, sobered; but it didn't chill his interest. He had seen farm animals bred before, but this was something different. He had never felt toward the cattle and sows on the farm this sense of compassion and tenderness. For the inmates of the Animal Store, he felt an empathetic joy in their natural respite from the cruelty, hunger, and filth in which they lived.

There was a feisty little chow-chow the marshal had picked up in the city in June, about the time Jody came to work. He was boarding the dog for the summer while the owner took a cruise in the Mediterranean. The chow was a fine dog with a pedigree, but he was useless for show because he had lost his left foreleg. The owner was one of those people who didn't care for the dog but didn't have the initiative or courage to have it killed. The chow had lived a pampered, dull life before coming under the marshal's care. The dog's name was Rupert Something-or-Other, and he didn't take any crap from anybody. The marshal tried the leather club and even a small chain, but never reduced Rupe to submission; therefore Rupe, as Jody called him, evoked hatred in the place of the usual indifference. Jody loved him.

When Jody took him to the bitch in heat, Rupe performed with a mastery that warmed the boy's heart. Rupe would hop up like a bull, short as his legs were, and hump away like a sewing machine. If the bitch were large she would have to squat a little. Rupe hung on fiercely with one good foreleg and a stump, while the battered old bitch hunkered and moaned in delight.

"Go to it, Boy," Jody said softly, reverently. "Go to it, old Girl. Good for you."

He thought about Rupe a lot, about what a shame he had lost a leg, but how proud and unwhipped he was. He thought of his own maimed young manhood, about his festering face, his body so skinny and unhandsome for all his young strength. Sometimes he likened himself to Rupe the cripple. Then again, he recognized the difference between them. He thought how unafraid Rupe was of the marshal, and how he no more grieved for his stump than if it were a sound whole leg. Rupe didn't care whether he was a show dog or not. Jody had to concede that the dog had long ago arrived at a state of acceptance which he himself must, somehow, learn.

There wasn't a girl in Trasherdell school that cared to be seen with him, he thought honestly, not even the homeliest. He tried out some tentative fantasies about the two or three most promising, but he was at once aware how illusory these fantasies were. It was not possible, unless he changed almost beyond recognition, that any girl or woman would ever be delighted with him. In a bittersweet, lonely ecstasy, with no rancor but only a sweet sad envy, he watched Rupe do his princely dance and cheered him on.

Chapter Two

The garbage run was over, the animals had been fed their scraps, and the other stuff had been buried in the big lot or was burning in the rusty barrel. Jody had nothing to do but "tidy up." That's what the marshal called the vague, endless, pointless routine by which, it was pretended, the store was made more orderly and clean. Jody understood, almost from the first day, that the marshal didn't care at all that the store was grimy and cluttered, didn't really see the filth and disorder. The assignment to tidy up was meant only to keep Jody working at something. The marshal didn't believe in paying a boy and letting him sit around.

Jody pushed his stub of a broom methodically across the oil–caked floor, back and forth, back and forth, not busily but unrestingly. He kept to the back corners out of the way of the knot of loafers who had gathered, as they did every day of the week, to waste the long summer afternoon.

They all sat with their chairs pulled around the cast–iron stove, though it was mid–July and the stove hadn't been lit since March, every chair or crate in its appointed crease in the floor. Johnny Burton was telling one of his long, raunchy stories, and everybody else was listening. They acted indifferent, but they were all quiet and attentive. Once in a while, a grunt or chuckle came out involuntarily. The indifference was all pretense. Johnny was a compelling yarn–spinner. He acted out the roles in his stories with gusto, and he had no inhibitions and no shame.

His stories were all crudely sexual. In them pretty girls or pretentious old maids were outwitted and divested by uncomely or unlikely but virile and clever horny males. Or, roles reversed, timid or dandified men were reclaimed to prurience by horny and clever females. The yarns were rich in pubic detail, full of physical and emotional cruelty, mutilations or suggestions of mutilation, plays on sexual ignorance or ineptitude or impotence. Johnny delivered them in a dazzling, creative vulgarity, arresting and poetic.

All this was clearly the devil's work, Jody knew, but he listened in spite of himself. The cruelty in the stories sent a pang through his abdomen and made his throat feel as if he would retch, just when everyone else was beginning to guffaw. He would succumb at last to the raw fascination of the story, and to Johnny's wizardry, and snort with the rest of them while his ears burned red and he wondered at himself.

This yarn was about animals, a farmer who had a pretty little mare to breed but didn't have the price for a stud. The farmer was trying to get someone with a stallion to let her be bred for free, in exchange for half the price the foal would bring. He had been to several of his neighbors, none of them willing to take his deal. He had come down the scale from racehorse to plowhorse to nag, and now as a last resort had led the pretty mare to old farmer Smith, who was as poor as he was but had an aged jackass that could still copulate.

"This old jack," said Johnny, hunching over and thrusting out his neck until his face seemed to lengthen and his big ears stuck out from his knotty head, "This old jack, you understand, he's nibblin cockleburs and sunflower, whatever he could find around the shithouse to eat, when he sees old farmer Jones leadin this pretty little filly up the path from the gate, and he ain't had nothin to hump fer two years but Smith's bony old jenny. And his old head rared up and his tail stuck up from his butt, and he started shufflin down to meet them, and he actually broke into a trot. And so all the time Jones was tryin to talk Smith into this deal, old Jack is a–shufflin round and round this filly, sniffin her up, tryin to nibble her titties, and he's gettin so horny he plumb forgets he's fifteen years old. So Smith was a–sayin to Jones, 'now how's that agin? You're gonna do what? Sell the mule colt and give me half of whatever you git?' And Jones says, 'shore, ain't that a good deal? Don't cost you nothin, and don't you think you'll need a few dollars a year from now?' And Smith is rubbin his jaw and thinkin, and then he says, 'Look, you go away with your bred mare and I ain't got no hold over you at all. What happens if you sell the colt and don't give me nothin? How am

I suppost to git my money, huh?' And now old Jack's been listenin to this conversation, and he don't like the way it's goin. So he jes sets back on his haunches with his old solger stickin up hard as a walnut limb, and he says, 'Aaaw– waaw–waaw–waw, Boss! HEEEE'll payuh! HEEEE'll payuh!'"

Johnny was squatted back on his heels, his forearms dangling between his knees, his neck stretched out and his face to the ceiling, making the room ring with the sound of his braying. It was startlingly realistic, as though the marshal had really picked up some unlucky farmer's jack and had him stabled just behind the wall. The loafers broke into long, raucous laughter and whoops; the judge sat on his swivel chair, his fat paunch shaking, tears running down his cheeks. The marshal himself was doubled over like a man with a cramp, his face distorted in ecstasy, all his bad teeth showing. Even Harry Bewley, whose face always had an ingrained sadness, who seldom spoke but sat hunched in his corner like a sick gipsy, was laughing, a coughing, painful laugh hardly distinguishable from sobbing. Johnny glowed quietly in this genuine praise. He took out his can of Prince Albert and a packet of papers and made himself a cigarette while the room slowly subsided.

Then Doc started sputtering again, laid back his fat face and said, "Aaaaaaw–waaaaw–waaaaw Boss!" The room erupted in laughter again. Johnny grinned in pleasure, and almost without hesitancy passed his can of P. A. and the papers to the marshal on his right. The marshal helped himself, shaking with laughter still, and passed them on. The can and papers went round the circle, and when they came back to Johnny the can was empty. He threw it ruefully into the barrel of litter in the corner.

They had been laughing so hard nobody had heard the car pull up outside, but when the door slammed they all looked around. There was Bill Becker's 1938 Buick, sleek and black as if it were new. Rose Becker got out of the driver's side and was coming around to help Bill. She had pulled up as close to the store as she could get and still have room to get him out. She opened his door, bent down, picked him up like a baby, and carried him inside. The judge jumped up quickly, and Rose plumped Bill down in the swivel chair where the judge had been.

Bill was a big man, not tall but muscular in the chest and arms and bloated in his abdomen and legs. Rose was a big Percheron of a woman who could have easily whipped anyone in the room. Even so, she was winded with the exertion and gladly sat down on the chair Doc offered her. Sweat stood in the creases under her eyes and chin and beaded her forehead and the scalp where it showed through her straw–blond hair.

"Whew!" Rose said. "Bill, honey, I don't know how much longer I'm gonna be able to lug you around everywhere we go. We're gonna have to get you a wheelchair, Darlin."

"Can't afford a damn wheelchair, Sweet Rose Baby," said Bill gruffly. "We just need to stay home more and not run around so much. 'Lo, Judge, Marshal. 'Lo, Doc, Johnny." He looked at Harry Bewley and nodded, but didn't say anything to him. "How you boys been?"

"We're all fine," said Harry, pretty loud, to everybody's surprise. "How you been yourself, old Billy? Ain't seen you in a year." He had stood when Rose came carrying Bill in, and now he came up and softly put a hand on Bill's shoulder.

"How the hell should a man be when he can't even take a shit by himself?" Bill said, turning his face away.

Johnny and the marshal snickered. Harry moved his hand from Bill's shoulder and backed off into his corner.

"Now, Bill," said Rose, "ain't no need to be talking like that. Don't pay him no mind, Harry honey. He's just cross today. You still got your old truck, you and Bill and me used to run round in before the war? Boy, didn't we have some good times, huh?"

"Sure, Rose," said Harry, his voice gentle. "We had good times."

"Didn't we have good times, Bill honey?" Rose said.

"Yeah. Let's get this business done, Sweet Rose Baby, and go. This place smells like dogshit."

There was a moment of silence. Then the marshal said, "What can I do fer you, Rose?"

"Marshal, I want to buy a puppy. I lost my dog Rex last week, and I'm lonely fer him and I want another dog." Rose's eyes began to water, and her lip was trembling. "You remember Rex, Harry? Me and Bill got Rex right after you went overseas. I sure loved that dog."

"I got some good dogs," the marshal said. "You need a grown one fer a watchdog, Rose."

"No, I want a puppy I can raise myself. I want one that will grow up to be a big dog, though, Marshal."

"Jody, go get them two pups from Nellie," the marshal said.

Jody stopped staring at Bill's abdomen, but not before Bill saw him staring, and went to Nellie's pen. She made no protest when Jody picked up her two surviving pups, simply thumped her tail on the hard dirt floor. Jody brought them, a male and a female, and after some hesitation put one on Bill's lap and gave the other into Rose's hands.

"Aw, ain't he pretty?" said Rose, lifting the pup to look at his underbelly. "Are they both male?"

As if to show she was not, the pup in Bill's lap squatted and peed generously. Bill wasn't looking at her and couldn't feel the wet, so he didn't know it until Johnny Burton whooped with laughter as he pointed to Bill's lap. Everybody in the room had a good roaring laugh, except for Bill, who didn't act like it was funny, and Jody, who was embarrassed and scared.

"Here, boy," said Bill, "take this one back to Nellie, whoever she is, and don't put no more dogs in my lap." He handed the pup to Jody.

Jody took it with his hands shaking. "I'm sorry," he said.

The effect of those words on Bill was immediate and startling. "Sorry, hell! What have you got to be sorry for? You didn't pee on me, did you? I'm not asking anybody to feel sorry, and that goes fer the whole fucking bunch of you. That goes fer you too, Harry Bewley, you bastard."

The room was quiet as death. Jody stood with the pup wiggling in his hands. "It ain't the pup's fault," Jody said.

"Shit, boy, I know that. Pups don't pee when they want to. They pee when they have to. Just like old paralyzed men, they don't pee when they want to, they pee when their bladder wants to. You think that's funny as hell, don't you?"

"That's enough, Bill," Harry said. "That boy didn't laugh at you. Nobody laughed at you. Take the pup away, Jody. Go on, now."

Jody hurried out of the room with the pup. He stuffed it into Nellie's cage again and hurried back to listen from outside the door.

"C'mon, now, Bill," Harry said. "Let it go. Don't make Rose feel bad. Let her enjoy her new puppy. I'm askin' you, let it go, fer old time's sake."

"You think you're something smart, don't you, Harry. I wish I had my legs back fer ten minutes. I'd get up out of this chair and whip your ass." He was silent for a while. Then he spoke more quietly. "C'mon, Rose. Pay the Marshal fer your dog, and let's go. How much you want fer the pup, Marshal?"

"Twenty dollars," the marshal said, his voice cold and steady.

Bill made no protest. "Pay him, Sweet Rose Baby."

"Bill, it's too much!"

"It's all right. Pay him."

Through the crack by the door hinge, Jody saw Rose fish a bill from her pocket and give it to the marshal.

"Now, let's go. Here, Rose, Sweetie, let me hold your puppy." Bill cradled the pup in one huge hand against his soiled paunch and put the other arm abound Rose's shoulder. She carried him back out to the seat of the car. Its door still stood open.

All the loafers were quiet. Doc and Judge took back their seats. Jody slipped back in, picked up his broom, and started sweeping again.

"You know, Harry," Johnny said with a wink at the marshal, "I think Rose has got an eye on you. I think you could get some of that, don't you reckon?"

There was a mild snicker from the marshal.

"I bet you could shuck some of old Bill's corn."

Harry sat quietly, looking moodily at the floor.

"Don't you think so, Harry?" Johnny insisted, grinning around at everyone else.

"Maybe so," Harry said.

"Well, then, why don't you get after it, huh? Ain't hurting old Billy's business, that's fer sure. He's done retired from that line of work."

There were a few half–hearted chuckles from the others, but Harry had the old sick look around his mouth and eyes again. He looked Johnny straight in the eye. Then he got up very deliberately and hit Johnny a resounding slap across the mouth.

"If you don't know why, Johnny, there's no way I can explain it." He spat leisurely on the marshal's stove, picked up his battered hat, and walked out into the afternoon sun. In a few seconds they heard his old truck start up.

"Well," said Johnny at last, "ain't that just the drizzlin shits?" His voice was strained, but he was struggling to recover. "A man smokes the last pinch of your tobacco and then can't take a little joke. Hell of a note." He got up and stretched self–consciously. "Now I got to get me some more PA and settle my nerves with a smoke, that is if I can roll one, fer my hands a–shakin."

Everyone chuckled politely to let Johnny know his courage was not in question. He sauntered out of the store, and even though the afternoon was still early, the others also began to shuffle and make signs of leaving.

The marshal put the bill in his dirty wallet and said to Jody, "You close the place up. I'm gonna take off."

Only the judge still sat in his swivel chair when the others were gone. Jody still swept his corner mindlessly, his heart in turmoil. The judge watched him quietly in the hot, smelly silence.

"Put that broom down, son, and come sit. Only a fool works when the boss has already quit and gone."

Jody propped the broom in the corner and sat down gingerly in the marshal's chair. It felt strange to be sitting there. He didn't want the judge to see him feeling that way, so he spat on the ground and put his feet up on the stove. There was only a flicker of a smile on the judge's lips, but Jody saw it and felt vaguely ashamed.

Over the past weeks the judge had been friendly, and Jody liked him better than any of the others. Sometimes the judge would say something to him, whereas the rest of the group usually acted like he wasn't there. Sometimes the judge would bring one of his books with him, and when everyone else had gone in the late afternoon, he would ask Jody to read to him. He said it hurt his old eyes to read very long.

Sometimes he brought a yellow magazine called National Geographic with luscious color pictures and fascinating articles. Once he brought a book of poems. Often Jody would get so absorbed in the reading he almost forgot the judge was there until he would look up and see the old man's eyes watching him intently.

"How much of all that did you understand?" the judge said.

"Not much," Jody said. "Mrs. Becker wanted a dog. She wanted a male dog. Seems like her and Harry and Mr. Becker used to be friends. Mr. Becker can't walk or—nothing. Seems like he don't like Harry anymore."

"Well," the judge said quietly, "you got most of it right, except for some details." He took a fresh cigar from his shirt pocket and lit it.

Jody waited a minute, but the judge didn't go on. He very much wanted to know more. Finally he said, "I wonder how Mr. Becker got paralyzed."

The judge took a long drag on the cigar and let the smoke come out slow and drift around his head. "He was hurt once."

"I reckon he don't like me much," Jody said. "I don't know what I did to make him mad at me. I didn't know I shouldn't give him the pup."

"He came down on you pretty hard, but there was nothing personal in it. You just happened to be there. It would have been the same for anyone else."

Jody waited patiently. At last the judge took a long pull at his cigar, laid it down on the edge of the stove, and looked at Jody.

"I don't know whether you can understand or not, but I'll try to explain." He leaned back in the chair and folded his hands behind his head.

"Bill and Harry worked together in the old days. They ran a bootlegging business in the city when they were still kids. The big boys ran them out of town, and they settled in Trasherdell. When prohibition was repealed, Oklahoma stayed dry, so business went on as usual. They made some good money. That's how Bill got that car. Boy, was he proud of that car.

"Whenever they weren't doing business, they helled around day and night. Rose was still a teenager when they started running around together, the three of them. She was Harry's girl, mostly, but the three of them were always together. They'd always be at some honky-tonk or tearing up and down the highway together at eighty miles an hour. They ran the highway patrol ragged. They never did anybody any harm, far as I know, except maybe get in a fight now and then. I remember they all three came to court once because they'd been trespassing. They tore down a farmer's fence and were out on his hay meadow in Harry's pickup, chasing jackrabbits with the headlights. The old man came to the sheriff next day, raising hell. I fined them twenty dollars, which was a big fine in those days. They all laughed. Bill threw down a ten, Harry threw down a ten, and then

Rose walked up and threw down a ten too. They thought that was really funny. They used to remind me of it every time they saw me.

"Then one night they got caught. Bill went into this house to deliver a bottle and it was a trap. They got old Bill dead to rights with the goods on him. Rose and Harry saw it was all up, and they took off in Bill's car."

"Is that why Bill doesn't like Harry?"

"No, that's not it. They all knew someone would get caught someday. Harry couldn't help Bill anyway. Harry and Rose were there at Bill's trial, and they were all friendly as ever. Bill went up to Big Mac to do a little time. Harry and Rose carried on business as usual, a little more carefully of course. It was all a calculated risk. I was the judge who sent Bill up. He doesn't hold a grudge against me, either.

"Then everything went wrong. Bill always had a smart mouth, and he didn't understand how to get along in the pen. One day this guy bumped his tray in the mess hall, and Bill said something smart to him. It happened to be Jake Huckaby. Jake was doing life for stomping his wife to death. There was a fight, only it wasn't much of a fight. Jake beat Bill into putty while everybody watched. The guards let it go on a little while to let Bill learn his lesson."

"That's what crippled him?"

The judge nodded slowly. "Jake broke his back. Bill spent the rest of his term in the prison hospital. Harry and Rose went to see him, but Harry never would go again. Rose would go up to see Bill every time she could, but Harry never would. Then Harry started drinking too much, and he and Rose split up. Then the war broke out, and Harry joined the army."

The judge was silent for a long time. Jody fidgeted quietly, then finally said, "So Rose and Bill got married."

The judge smiled wryly. "They had the chaplain come up to Bill's hospital room. Rose asked me to come to the ceremony. By that time I wasn't a judge any more. I didn't know why she wanted me there, but I felt sorry for her, so I went. I guess I felt sorry for Bill too. And Harry. Anyway, I went. Harry didn't come. Said he couldn't get a pass. I don't know whether that was true or not. Well, the chaplain said his 'dearly beloved' and Rose and Bill said 'I do,' and Rose bawled and bawled. I really wanted to get away. After the ceremony, the chaplain left, and there were just the three of us.

"Rose wanted to tell all over again how she and Bill and Harry paid that twenty–dollar fine. She kept asking me did I remember it. I said several times yes I did, and we all tried to laugh about it together. I didn't like being in that room. I kept thinking it was Bill's hospital room but also their honeymoon room, or as close to one as they'd ever have. It made me kind of sick. Finally I got away."

Jody listened carefully, trying to take it all in. There were so many things to think about, and he couldn't keep track of them all. There were questions he wanted to ask, but couldn't find any way to put them into words. Out of all this welter of feelings and ambiguities, he chose one.

"Why should Bill—Mr. Becker, I mean—be mad at Harry? Is it because he didn't come to the wedding?"

"No, son, not exactly. As a matter of fact, he isn't really mad at Harry at all, though maybe he thinks he is. He's ashamed." The judge looked thoughtfully at his cigar, now grown cold, laid it on the floor and crushed it with his heel.

"He wasn't mad at you, either. I wanted you to understand that, maybe because I sent him to prison and there he got himself messed up. Mind you, there wasn't anything wrong about what I did, but I can't help feeling guilty about it, anyway. I wanted you to know that Bill Becker is not a cruel man, not yet, anyway." The judge stood up slowly. "That's why I can't be a judge anymore. I think too much about why people really do things that are criminal. Anyway, Bill never meant to hurt anybody. Now, you take that Jake Huckaby. That's a cruel man."

"And the marshal," Jody said, almost to himself, before he thought.

The judge looked at him strangely, his hand pausing with his hat halfway to his head. "Cruel people are mostly just scared or hurt. Some of them, though, get to like being cruel." He put his hat on and waddled slowly out.

That left Jody alone with the animals and a riot of strange feelings. He walked up and down among their cages, talking to them and petting them gently. He got the water bucket and made the full round, filling all their watering cans with cool water, even the ones that were still full. Finally he made out his bedroll in the corner of the office. He ate a little bread and cold gravy from the food the marshal had brought him, then lay down on the pallet. It was still light out, and he couldn't sleep.

Chapter Three

He lay there for nearly an hour, image after image rolling through his mind, Johnny's story and the fight at the pen and the little she–dog squatting on Bill's paunch making a slow stain. He couldn't fix on any of it. His mind tumbled everything randomly as his body squirmed and flopped on the hot, hard bed.

At last he got up, pulled on his overalls and shoes, and let himself out by the back door. He stuck a board in the door so it wouldn't close and lock him out, then vaulted the hog–wire fence. It was early evening, still hot, still light. A bloodred full moon was pulling itself free from the horizon, but the western sky was still ablaze. The street was deserted. In kitchen windows he saw men in undershirts seated at the supper table, or the women bent over washing dishes. He saw little groups on porches, smoking and talking. Some of the boys he knew were working on a dismantled Chevy. But Jody didn't want to talk to anyone. He hurried on by as if on an errand, moving randomly through alleys and lots, moving instinctively toward the open country, away from people.

Without really going anywhere in particular, he saw he was on the edge of the town where the houses became spread out in small acreages. Finally he came to a house twenty acres away from anyone, knowing suddenly he had wanted to come here from the first. It was a little clapboard, rundown house with high weeds all around, except for a rock–hard bare spot close by the front door where Rose Becker always parked the Buick so she wouldn't have to carry Bill very far.

The car wasn't there, so he knew the house was empty. Slowly, slowly he walked up the long dive. In his abdomen there was a strange, sick longing he couldn't really name. He felt like an intruder, but he had to know about Bill and Rose. He wasn't just curious; he craved, needed, to understand it all.

The house was weathered, unkept. Window screens were hanging loose, the rust from them running down the gray walls in patterns as if the eyes of the house had wept. Nails also had rusted and pulled loose from the clapboards, standing out naked and stained from the boards, with a tiny round rusty depression where they had once been hammered in. There were last–year's wasp's nests clinging to the eaves. Where the boards met the weedy earth, they were rotting and feathery. The last light of the western sky reflected from the panes, and his own dark image looked back at him. Nothing of the dark mystery inside revealed itself, although, frightened at his own daring, he put his forehead up against a window screen trying to see.

Slowly he walked around the house, feeling as though the ghost of old Rex might stand up suffering from some hidden grave and bare his yellow teeth. He pushed his way into the weed–grown backyard. Obviously nobody came there, except along the well defined path to the sagging outhouse where the weeds stretched away to blend into a fallow, gullied field.

The house was shaped like a box with the two rooms or maybe three in a straight row. It was what the old–timers called a shotgun house. A lean–to room had been added on the backside, barely six feet high where the slope of its roof ended. Where it joined on, the clapboards had fallen loose from the wall and were resting on the lean–to roof.

Jody looked round him furtively, then impulsively he put one foot on a decaying window sill and pulled himself up onto the lean–to. There, belly down on the wooden shingles, he examined the opening in the wall left where the clapboards had been.

Years of rain and snow had trickled through aging shingles, run down behind the wall, and softened the clapboards until they had dropped from their nails by their own weight. The studs and rafters were beginning to rot too, and behind them the exposed inner wall of sheet rock was stained and soft–looking. There was a crack as wide as his finger where the wall joined the ceiling. Jody could feel it under the edges of the aged shingles.

Still not really thinking about it, he carefully tugged at the overhanging shingles until he had worked three of them loose.

Where they had been, the crack in the inner wall lay exposed. By pulling himself up close and laying his head where the shingles used to be, Jody could look through the crack to the room below. The crack wasn't caused by the weather, as he had supposed, but by the carelessness or deliberate economy of the builders. The panels of the ceiling weren't quite wide enough to cover the room, and had been left scant. The crack ran all along the room, probably ran the whole length of the house.

He was looking from one corner into a shabby, poorly furnished bedroom. There was an old bedstead with a sagging mattress covered with a rumpled, worn quilt. Beside the bed was a heavy wooden chair with a big hole cut in the seat. A battered dishpan rested on the floor directly under the chair. A few clothes, Bill's clothes, hung in an open–faced closet. Some dog–eared magazines lay on the floor by the bed, and there was a table with a radio on the side opposite the chair. On the table by the radio was a washbasin, shaving mug, straight razor, comb, stand–up mirror, and some few other toiletries, not recognizable. In the gathering dusk, he could see nothing more.

He studied the room carefully, imagining the uses to which each object was put, seeing in his mind the paralyzed man hauling himself by his arms from the bed to the commode, lying by the hour thumbing the old magazines or idly listening to the radio. Slowly a shame suffused him. What was he doing here? What did he think he would see? What right had he to look on Bill's misery so? What would he say if he were discovered? He breathed deeply. This was altogether a different thing from watching Rupe and the bitches.

He heard the Buick pulling into the yard on the other side of the house. His shame turned to panic. He was on the verge of clambering down and running, but realized it was too late to do that without the risk of being caught. He flattened himself against the roof and lay still.

He heard the noises of Rose carrying Bill out of the car, then the outside door of the room opened below and Rose, straining and huffing, lugged Bill into the room and set him on the commode. Bill once more held the puppy cradled against his paunch.

"Gee, I'm sorry, honey. We should have known not to go driving so long. It's all my fault," Rose said. She was tugging at Bill's trousers, pulling them down over his huge hips and lifting his legs to take them off over his feet. "Now don't you mind. I'll clean everything up before no time."

Bill said nothing, but Jody thought he seemed to be crying softly in the darkening room.

"Here, give me the puppy now, and I'll get a light." She took the dog and the trousers and underclothes in a wad out of the room.

Bill sat forlornly as the puppy started to whine elsewhere in the house. That meant she had put him down somewhere to tend her other duties. After a few minutes, Bill rubbed his face, then pulled off his shirt and undershirt so he sat naked except for his shoes. He took a nightshirt from under the quilt, put it over his head, put his arms through the sleeves, and then spread it as best he could over his paunch and knees.

"There now, Darlin," Rose said, coming back into the room with a kerosene lamp and a pan of water. The puppy was still whining somewhere. "Let's get you cleaned up and into bed." In the soft lamp-light below, uneven shadows danced in the corners of the room.

"Oh, Rosie Baby, it's gonna be a bad night," Bill said, his voice husky. "I wisht we hadn't seen old Harry. Brought all of it back. I just can't stand it sometimes, you know, Baby?"

"I know, Hon, I know," she said, standing behind his chair, leaning over him and wrapping her huge arms around his head. She rocked his head in her arms, pressed against her big breasts, rocked him and soothed him like a baby. They stayed so in silence a long time. At last Jody saw Bill's hand steal up and caress Rose's face.

She took the basin and a rag and kneeled in front of him. She took off his shoes and socks, then washed his legs and genitals and paunch. Then she stood beside him while he pulled himself upright, hanging on her neck. She helped him lie forward on the bed, the huge buttocks gleaming in the lamplight. Jody turned away, sick, as Rose began to wash, but he could hear the water splash intermittently as she rinsed the rag, and through that sound the other sounds of Bill's soft sob in a continuum, punctuated by the low soothing tones of Rose's voice in words Jody couldn't understand. Then the sounds changed. He heard Rose going out. The bed creaked and groaned. When he looked again, Bill was lying on his back, staring at the ceiling. He had stopped crying, and his face in the lamplight was like a dead man's in repose.

31

"Now, Darlin," Rose said, coming back, "I'm gonna get you somethin to eat, and then we can listen to the radio together. We'll turn a bad time into a good time, you'll see." She bent over and kissed his face.

"Never mind, Sweet Rose Baby, I ain't hungry," Bill said softly, laying his hand on her knee. She sat down beside him on the commode and took his hand. "I just need you to be here by me a little, and then I'll go to sleep. Lord only knows how I love you, Baby," he went on clumsily. "Makes it hard to think what a trouble I am to you all these years."

"Hush, now," Rose said gently. "Hush now."

"No, I need to say some things," Bill said. "I need to say I'm sorry for that, sweet Rose." He lifted her hand up to his face and caressed himself with her fingers, then kissed them softly. After a few moments, he went on.

"I need you to do something fer me, tomorrow or the next day or whenever you see Harry again. I want you to tell him I'm sorry for what I said to him today. I didn't mean anything by it. Harry's been our good friend, hasn't he, sweet Rose? Do you think he feels we did him wrong?"

"I think he feels all right towards us," said Rose, big tears rolling down her flushed, horsy face. "He was real friendly today, you know? Harry's our friend, Bill honey. You need to tell him yourself, if you want to."

"I know," Bill said. "Maybe I'll do that soon as I see him again. I want you to go ahead and tell him fer me anyway, sweet Rose, whenever you see him next."

"Sure, Honey. Sure."

Bill wiped his eyes with his other hand. "That's a good kid the marshal has got working fer him. I shouldn't of talked to him that way. That's the kid that come by when Rex was sick, ain't he, Josh Carpenter's boy? What's his name?"

"Jody. Sure, that's Josh's boy."

"Maybe the best man I ever knowed, Josh Carpenter. He was a real friend when we didn't have many. I'm sorry I talked mean to that boy. You tell him that fer me."

"Sure," Rose said. "But why not you, Bill?"

Bill closed his eyes. "I'm no good at saying such things. You, now, you can say fer me. You're good and gentle talking. You're my good old Rose." A slight smile stayed on his face a moment, but he didn't open his eyes. "And another thing. You've got to forgive me for all of it, Rose. I need to hear you say it, say you forgive everything, all the bad I've caused you."

"Now, Bill, damn it—"

"And all I'm gonna cause in the future. C'mon, Rose. I need to hear it."

She laid her head over on his chest and bawled heartily. After a while, she got her sobs under control, sat up, and wiped her eyes. She took his hand between hers. "All right, Bill, if you want me to, though you know good and well— Sure, Honey, I forgive everything, whatever."

Then the room was quiet for a while, except for a snuffle or two from Rose.

"Thanks, sweet Baby. Now I've got to go to sleep."

Rose sighed a little, but she didn't rise or let go his hand. "Bill," she said at last, "do you think we could try again?"

"Now Rose, what's the good of that? You know I can't do you no good. I ain't never gonna do you no good." There was a harsh note in his voice.

"We could play like, couldn't we? Wouldn't that make you feel better, maybe?" She lifted his hand and held it against a breast. "I think it might make us both feel better, you know? Please, Bill," she said gently. "Let's try."

She stood beside his bed. To Jody's amazement she whipped her dress over her head in one quick movement and tossed it aside. In another two seconds she had shucked her undergarments. She took Bill's nightshirt in both hands and pulled it up around his armpits. Below his prominent paunch and graying pubic hair, his penis lay small and limp. She knelt on his bed, fondling him with her right hand. With her left, she took his hand and laid it on her crotch.

"Oh God, Rose," Bill said, caressing her in spite of himself. He pulled her body upon him so she sat across his fork. As she rocked and moaned, he cupped his hands around her breasts, his eyes closed, a look of agony on his face.

For perhaps two minutes she writhed and hunched, moaning softly. Then she stopped. Her broad shoulders began shaking, and she sobbed heavily. She leaned over and laid her body close on his, crying uncontrollably. Bill's upper torso heaved and writhed, his hands massaging her back and buttocks, until slowly his arms relaxed, and he too wept.

When they were both quiet, she got up from the bed, pulled the nightshirt down over his body, and softly, still naked, took his face in her hands and kissed him. "I'm sorry, Bill," she said, her voice broken.

"Yeah. Me too, Baby," Bill said almost inaudibly.

Rose picked up her clothes, took the lamp with her, and went out, closing the door. Only a little moonlight was left in the room, falling across the swell of Bill's belly.

Jody lay motionless. He was drenched with sweat. Slowly, ever so carefully, he detached several shingles from the left of the hole where his head lay. Sure enough, he could now see into the adjoining room. He laid the shingles noiselessly beside him with the others, shifted his body carefully, and looked into the bedroom of Rose Becker.

It was really the living room, almost as spare as Bill's room, with a couch that made into a bed. Rose was sitting, still naked, on the couch, crying softly to herself. The lamp sat on the floor in front of her, illuminating her broad body. The puppy whined softly from a cardboard box at her side. Without even looking at him, she picked him up and cuddled him between her overripe breasts, stroking him gently. Then she stopped crying and held him up before her with her left hand—as she had in the store, Jody remembered. With her right hand she began to fondle his belly. Slowly she stretched her body backward on the couch. Then, her abdomen rising and falling rhythmically, with one hand holding the pup in place between her breasts, she reached over, pulled the lamp up to her face, and blew out the light.

Struggling to control his shaking hands, Jody took up the shingles he had removed and one by one pushed them softly back into the room from where they had come. Then, slowly, quietly, he inched his way down the lean-to roof, felt carefully for the window sill with his foot, and let himself back down among the weeds. Stealthily he crept around the house, past the black Buick gleaming in the moonlight, softly down the long drive, making himself keep to the turf so he wouldn't be heard. Once in the road he ran, almost all the way to the store, until he thought that would seem strange to anyone who saw him. Then he hurried to the fenced lot, climbed over the fence, let himself in where he had left the door ajar, and sank gratefully on the hard, smelly pallet he had left two hours before.

He lay with his heart beating wildly, his eyes wide open, staring into the gloom made by the moonlight through dirty windows, his mind racing, the images of the day and night passing like a kaleidoscope. Little by little he quieted; little by little it all began to settle into an order. Gone now was the yearning curiosity, and in its place was an awed sadness. One by one he thought of the people who had figured in the day. One by one he sorted out their anguish, and thought their stories through.

He arose again, propped open the back door, and this time turned to the animal pens. In the soft moonlight, he found Rupe and spoke to him quietly. Rupe acknowledged him with a wag of the handsome tail curved over his rump. Jody sat a long time beside his pen, and the boy and dog sat looking into each other's faces. Rupe lay with his head erect, his stump laid across his good foreleg. His gaze was steady and regal. After a long time, calmed in mind, Jody rose and went back to his pallet.

Quieter now, he cried awhile about what he had seen. Then prompted by the training of his childhood, he rose again, slumped down on his knees beside the dirty pallet in the Marshal's Animal Store, and prayed. First he prayed his traditional prayer, asking a blessing on his mother and dad and Tommy. Then he asked forgiveness for himself for watching Bill and Rose. Then he asked a blessing on Rose Becker and Bill Becker and Harry Bewley and Judge Hanks and Doc White. After a little effort, he asked a blessing on Johnny Burton. He had to struggle a while because he wasn't sure Johnny wanted to be blessed. Then he decided it didn't make any difference as far as his prayer was concerned. It was only after he had lain down again, and thought about them for a long time, that at last he got up, knelt again, and asked a blessing on the marshal and the marshal's wife and Jake Huckaby. Then he lay down and slept at last.

Chapter Four

"Come on, boy," the marshal said. "Get up and get your clothes on. There's some boiled eggs in the sack, but you better eat fast 'cause it's time to work them garbage cans. You can't sleep all day, you know. Them animals has to eat too."

All the events of the previous evening came back in a rush, as if they had been waiting alert but motionless around his pallet to pounce on him at the first moment of consciousness. He lay absolutely still while his mind whirred with images and feelings, reliving all of them almost simultaneously. Then he began to orient himself. It was morning. For the first time, he had slept right through the dawn. Never before had the marshal not found him awake and ready for the work of the day.

Without a word he pulled on his overalls and shoes, almost as quickly as Rose had unclothed herself last night. The sun pushing in through the dirty windows of the store fell across the marshal's humped back as the moonlight had fallen on Bill's gown–clad torso. The battered telephone at the marshal's elbow and the coffee cup beside it took on the contours of the toiletries on the little table beside Bill's bed. In the pens outside, Nellie's remaining puppy was whining.

He opened the sack. There were three boiled eggs, five pieces of scorched toast, and a large scabby apple—his sustenance for the day. Quickly he cracked and peeled one egg, took it down in three bites, and folded a piece of toast into his mouth. He then picked up the watering bucket and took four long gulps. He was still hungry, but that would have to do. He had to leave something for the rest of the day. Besides, the marshal, seeing Jody was finished, had already started for the door.

The marshal fired up the truck, and Jody clambered into the back with the oil drums. He used to ride up front with the marshal when they would both get out and empty the garbage cans. After a week, Jody was hopping out to get the garbage while the marshal stood there and told him how to sort it. Now, the marshal stayed in the cab and drove. Jody picked up the stuff and sorted it himself, hopping up and down out of the pickup bed. When he finished at a stop, he slapped the top of the cab. The marshal, never looking around, drove on to the next cluster of cans.

Jody lifted two cans at a time, one with each hand wrapped in a handle, using an elbow against the side of the can for leverage, and set them up in the bed of the truck. Then he vaulted up between them and apportioned their contents expertly to the four drums. The rhythms and sounds and smells became automatic. He welcomed them for their distraction from the grim scenes his mind was trying to play over and over.

Nevertheless, hard as he tried not to think, the truck was coming nearer and nearer in their rounds to the clapboard house on the edge of town. Jody steeled himself for the ordeal of grief, played it out in his mind beforehand, prepared himself to work methodically, step by step. I'll jump down, with my back to the house, then . . . .

They were near. Jody had turned his back to the cab, looking behind him down the narrow, hard–packed dirt street becoming two bare tracks with the weeds growing between. Before they got there, he heard the marshal shout.

"Hey! What the hell is this?"

He turned around quickly and caught the whole scene at once, the worn house, the Buick where it had been, the weathered shingle roof. Huddled by the garbage can near the road, Rose sat wrapped in an old blanket, rocking slowly, eyes blank, mouth dropped open. It looked like the blanket was all she had on.

The marshal stopped the truck right in front of Rose and slowly opened the door, the hinges creaking. He stepped out on the running board, gawking at Rose across the hood.

"What the hell you doing out here, Rose, with no clothes on?" he asked.

Rose tried to answer him, but the words wouldn't come out. She swallowed a couple of times, and then said, slow and throaty, "I knew you'd come. I knew you'd be here." The rocking motion intensified. Jody had a flash of her broad back as she rocked and writhed astraddle Bill's motionless trunk. Suddenly she stopped, slumped, put her face on her knees. "He's up there." She waved vaguely at the house. "I can't go back."

Jody and the marshal exchanged a blank look, then hurried to the house. The door sagged on its hinges, standing nearly wide open, its panels broken and sticking outward. They stepped inside.

The blood pounded at Jody's temples. It was the same scene, but different. There was the commode, the crude pan, the table, the sagging bed with Bill in a mound. All, all there, with the sunlight glaring where the moon had shone and the lamplight and shadows had played softly on harsh features. All, all there, and all, all wrong. Involuntarily he raised his eyes. Along the ceiling at the back of the room, half an inch wide, there was a dark strip where the sheet–rock panel wasn't wide enough to reach the wall.

There was something else, something about the Bill thing mounded on the bed. Too still, too sprawled, one arm thrown outward, hanging stiffly off the edge. There was a huge red pattern around Bill's head and shoulders on the dingy quilt, like a halo, like a big rosy flower grotesquely adorning the sheet he lay on. More red on the right hand flung out from the bed. Near the hand, the straight razor, blade open.

"My God," said the marshal. He approached Bill gingerly, standing way back and peering over at him. "Damn near cut his head off. Somebody's broke in and butchered him like a hog."

Jody took one long, direct look at the gaping slash below Bill's chin, with Bill's wide–open, reproving eyes boring into his own. Then he turned and ran full tilt through the door, full force into the side of the Buick. The impact knocked him flat and dazed him. Through the bruising pain, his mind cleared. He sat up slowly, his head aching, dizzy, sick. He pulled himself upright by the handle of the car door.

The marshal looked at Jody intently, and seemed, himself, to snap out of his trance. "Well," he said, "nothing to do here right now." He came out and tried to close the broken door, but it dragged badly. So he lifted it on its hinges and pushed it as nearly shut as it would go. He did it gently, as if not to wake Bill Becker.

Soberly they walked back to the truck where Rose sat silently rocking back and forth. For a brief while they stood looking at her.

"We got to get her inside somewhere," Jody said at last.

"Yeah," the marshal said. "You go up to the house and get her some clothes. I'll run over to get Widow Gamble to look after her." Half–distracted, he climbed in the truck and drove off, too fast, swinging a wide, jouncing arc through the weeds, the green drums dancing in the back.

Jody didn't want to go back to the house, and he didn't want to leave Rose sitting by herself beside her garbage. He leaned over her and touched her shoulder. "You wait here, Miss Rose. Don't you be afraid." He didn't know whether she heard him or not.

He set his teeth and made himself walk rapidly back to the house. He went in the other door this time, into the room Rose slept in. The lamp was still sitting on the floor by the couch. The puppy was whining gently in its box. He found some dresses hanging on a rod against the wall, snatched the first one he came to, picked up her shoes. About to leave, he impulsively picked up the puppy.

He handed her the puppy first. She took it absently and sat helplessly cradling it. When she took it in her hands, the blanket fell away from her shoulders in a heap around her thighs. Hurriedly Jody tried to get her into the dress. He had to stuff in an arm at a time. She didn't seem to know what he was doing, but shifted the puppy from arm to arm and gave him her limbs to dress, like a child. The dress buttoned all down the front. He fumbled hurriedly to tug it over her large breasts, pulled it taut around her flanks, buttoned it carefully, trying to avoid touching her pelvis as he gingerly pulled the last button through its opening. There was nothing at all under the dress, and it gapped all down the front. Finished buttoning, he pulled the blanket back around her to hide the spots of flesh and hair between the buttons. She let him put her shoes on her bare feet.

By this time the truck was coming back, too fast, bouncing wildly on the uneven road. Mrs. Gamble, white–faced, was in the truck with the marshal. Among the three of them they got Rose into the truck between the marshal and Mrs. Gamble. Jody climbed in the back and hung on tight as the truck made its jouncing circle again. In a few minutes they had Rose in Mrs. Gamble's bed, and the old lady was trying to get her to drink some coffee.

They didn't finish the garbage run, but drove straight back to the store. The first shock was over now, and the marshal was beginning to feel the importance of his office. "I'll need to start an investigation," he said.

Even Jody knew it was the first investigation of his career.

Nobody was at the store but Johnny Burton. He was leaning his crate back against the wall, rolling a cigarette from a full can of Prince Albert, full of banter as always. That stopped soon enough. The marshal simply cut him off.

"Can't bother with that right now, John. I've got a murder on my hands I've got to investigate."

"Yeah?" said Johnny. His crate came down flat on the floor.

"Bill Becker. Throat cut wide open."

Johnny's eyes bugged. He dropped the cigarette and let it lie. The marshal, for all his hurry, took time to go back over the events of the morning for Johnny's sake. Some of the details were a little elaborated, Jody thought.

Johnny's imagination seemed fired too. He asked a few suggestive questions, drawing the marshal out. He had to hear the story three times. Johnny wasn't used to sitting so long, listening to someone else's story. Once he got it all in his head, he began to take charge of the conversation.

"Well," he said, "I guess I ain't surprised all that much. Bill always did make folks mad. That's how he got all broken up at the pen, wasn't it? I guess I wouldn't be surprised to hear the name of the guy who done it, neither. I bet you wouldn't be too surprised yourself, Marshal, now would you?" He leaned the crate backward again, and took out another paper and his tobacco.

"Well . . . no, I think I wouldn't," said the marshal. He looked puzzled, but he was trying to sound knowing. "Uh—what guy do you mean?"

"Why," said Johnny, letting the pretense stand, "the only guy with a motive. The only guy with anything to gain by old Bill's death. The guy Bill threatened to whip yesterday, and the guy he shamed in public. The guy he stole his wife from."

"Harry?" the marshal said incredulously. He looked at Johnny, dumbfounded, for nearly a minute, then began walking back and forth behind his desk, hands in pockets. "Why, sure. Harry."

Jody's heart was pounding, and a voice inside him was shouting No! No! but he couldn't say a word. Terrified, he heard a caustic laughter echoing somewhere in a deep cavern inside himself.

There was a shuffling and a muttering outside the door. Judge Hanks and Harry Bewley came in together talking, stopping as they always did for their morning coffee. Johnny and the marshal exchanged a startled look. Then the marshal walked deliberately from behind the desk and positioned himself in a formal stance by the stove. Harry and the judge broke off their conversation to stare at him.

"What is it?" the judge said. "What's the matter?"

"Harry Bewley!" the marshal announced as though he had practiced before a mirror, "I arrest you in the name of the law!" At the last word he pulled his gun from its holster and jabbed it toward Harry's chest.

"What're you doing?" Harry said. "Put that thing up, you damn fool, before it goes off."

The Marshal stood there like a cardboard Gene Autry in front of a movie theater. Harry's hand leaped out and took the gun. One instant the marshal was pointing it at Harry, then before Jody could blink, it lay snugly in Harry's hand. Harry flipped open the chamber, shook out the cartridges into his palm, and handed the gun back to the marshal.

"Now, what's this all about?" said Harry.

The marshal stood looking at his gun in his hand. He didn't look at Harry. "I'm arresting you for murder," he said weakly.

Harry sat down. "Murder?" He looked at the marshal in stunned disbelief. "Who?"

"Bill Becker. He's laying up there on his bed with his throat cut."

"Bill!" Harry said, almost a whisper. A big tear welled in each eye. "The poor son of a bitch." He sat silent, briefly. "Where's Rose?"

"She's at the Widow Gamble's," said the marshal. "Me and Jody took here there."

"I got her some clothes," Jody said, before he thought.

Harry turned and looked at him. It seemed like the man was looking into him, searching something there he hadn't expected to find. "Thank you, son," he said.

"Do you mean," the judge said, "that Bill's still lying up there in an empty house by himself?"

"That's right," said the marshal doggedly. "I've got to finish my investigation." Recovered, he reached over and took the cartridges from Harry's hand. "While I do, Harry, I'm going to lock you up."

"Where are you going to put him," the judge said, "in a chicken–wire cage?"

The marshal looked startled. Obviously he hadn't thought it all out yet, but he bluffed on through. "Yes," he said. He turned to the desk and took out a rusty set of handcuffs. "Come on, Harry."

He took Harry by the shoulder. Harry made no resistance. The marshal pushed him out into the old garage. There he stopped for a minute, searching a place. Then he steered Harry down the steps into the grease pit, and handcuffed him to the frame of one of the flimsy cages there. Although he was a little man, Harry had to sit on the floor, he was tethered so close.

Harry looked up at the marshal, who was climbing out of the pit. All around Harry were caged cats and wild creatures. "You don't know what you're doing."

The marshal propped the door into the garage wide open. Then he went back into the office.

"Marshal, listen to me," said the old judge. "You're in over your head. You need some help from somebody who's seen a murder before. Why don't you call the sheriff and ask him to come down here?"

"Not till I've done my own investigation," said the marshal stubbornly. He went to the desk, took out a pencil and some grimy paper, and started for the door. Abruptly he stopped, wheeled around, and said to Jody, "Keep an eye on the prisoner!" Then he went out the door and climbed into the old truck.

"You don't even know what you're looking for," the judge yelled at him.

The truck started and rumbled off.

The judge looked at Johnny, then Jody, then back at Johnny. "This is stupid! I wonder what put the fool notion in his head that Harry did it?" He walked to the door and looked down at Harry in the grease pit. "You all right?"

"Yeah, I'm all right," Harry said, "but I ain't going to sit here with this menagerie more than about three days."

"Now don't do anything dumb. One stupid citizen is enough in this establishment."

He paced up and down the office a turn or two, looking at Jody, looking at Johnny. Then, with a sigh, he sat down at the marshal's desk, picked up the telephone, and spun the dial one time. "Marge, get me the sheriff's office in Ashton."

"What do you think you're doing?" Johnny said.

The judge ignored him. "Hello, Lonnie. This is Joe Hanks over in Trasherdell. Fine, fine, I'm fine. Listen, Lonnie, this is business. We've got a killing over here, maybe a murder. Yeah. Think you'd better get over here right away. The marshal's on the scene, looking around, if you understand me. Yeah. It's Bill Becker, paralyzed man. You know him. He did a stretch in MacAlester once. Lives in a little house on the west side of town, off the highway north. Oh, Lonnie, one thing. Could you call the funeral home and ask them to send a hearse. Yeah. Well, I'll pay for it myself if I have to. Okay. I'll meet you here at the marshal's office. See you in a bit." Thoughtfully, he put the receiver down.

"Marshal ain't gonna like that," Johnny said.

"Shut up," the judge said.

"Hey, Jody," Harry said. "Come here, boy, will you?"

Jody hurried out and looked down into the pit.

"Listen, son, I'm worried about Rose. Think you could find Doc and tell him to look in on her?"

"Sure," Jody said. He started off, then turned back. "You've got to promise me you won't come out while I'm gone."

In spite of everything, Harry grinned. "Don't worry, son, I promise."

Jody finally found Doc leaving Art's Cafe where he had got his breakfast. He told him about Bill and Rose, standing in the middle of Main Street, watching the old man's face get pasty and grim as the story came out.

Doc said "Oh my God" then listened silently. He nodded when Jody told him what Harry wanted of him, and was climbing in his dusty Chevy coupe while Jody was still talking.

"You tell him I'll take care of it," he said, then drove off fast, leaving Jody standing in the street.

By the time he got back to the store, the sheriff's car with its red spotlight and a big shield on the door was already sitting outside. Jody had never seen it before and couldn't resist putting his hand out to touch his own disproportioned image in its shiny hood. As quietly as he could, he slipped in the door. The sheriff was talking in low tones with the judge. Johnny was nowhere around. They both looked up at Jody, but went on talking. Jody hurried out to the garage to tell Harry that Doc was on his way to Rose.

Harry was sitting with his head hanging down, but he nodded to let Jody know he understood. "Thanks, son," he said, but he didn't look up.

Jody edged back into the office. The sheriff looked at him keenly. He was a tall, lean man with a shock of iron gray hair and a hooked nose dominating his long, narrow face. When he spoke, his voice was a rich bass, full of sounds like the low notes of the organ at church.

"Come over here, son, and sit down. I want you to tell me everything you can remember about what happened this morning."

Jody sat on a crate, feeling fidgety. He had a wild impulse to spill all of it, the trip he had made to the Beckers' house the night before, his own sense of guilt. He didn't, though. He merely began his account with the discovery of Rose. The sheriff listened intently, never taking his black eyes off Jody for an instant. As Jody was finishing his story, he heard the marshal's truck rattle up outside. He tried not to think about what Johnny had said about the marshal not being pleased.

"All right, son," the sheriff said. "You did just fine. Now I'm going to need you after a while. We need to go back over some of this when I've been up there myself."

While he was talking, the marshal came in. He looked at Jody much as he had when Jody had challenged him about whipping the bitch, but he didn't speak to him. "Couldn't wait, could you?" he said to the judge.

The judge didn't bother answering.

"Well, Marshal," the sheriff said, "I hear you've got a killing in your town."

"That's right, Sheriff," the marshal said, not real friendly. "I've got me a killer, too."

"Is that right?" said the sheriff. "That's pretty fast work. How do you know Harry's a killer? By the way, how do you know it's a murder?"

"If you'd of seen old Bill Becker, you'd know it wasn't no accident," the marshal said, and chuckled grimly at his own joke. He took a plug of tobacco from his pocket, bit off a corner, and ceremonially sat down in the judge's swivel chair.

The sheriff waited for him to go on, but the marshal just mouthed his tobacco. The sheriff waited about a minute, then sighed deeply and said, "Let's see what you've got."

The marshal nodded. Then, deliberately, he took a piece of grimy paper from his pocket.

"First off," he said, importantly, "the house was broke into. The door is broke down and the lock has split out the frame where it was forced." He paused to let the words soak in.

Jody could read across the top of the paper "forsabul entry,"

The sheriff listened, his eyes boring into the marshal.

"That means someone broke in and killed him," the marshal explained condescendingly. He returned the sheriff's stare. When he was satisfied his point had taken, he turned to his notes again.

"Now about the motive," he said. "It wasn't robbery, cause I found the house wasn't ransacked and there was money still in the pockets of the clothes in the other room. Also the car keys. The car wasn't took."

There was another pregnant pause.

"Nope, it was a crime of passion. Rose wasn't hurt. Whoever did it wanted to take something out on Bill. It was somebody that had something to settle." He paused and spat deliberately in the bucket.

"It was somebody small." Here he paused for fully thirty seconds and looked triumphantly into the sheriff's motionless eyes. "The intruder cased the house afore he broke in. Walked all the way around it. I seen where he walked through them tall weeds in back. He left a trail like a cow in a sorghum patch. You could tell where his feet sot down."

He paused and chewed slowly, while Jody's heart thumped as though it would jump from his body.

"Had a short stride," he said to the sheriff, deliberate and emphatic, as though explaining to a child.

"Now about the modus operandi," the marshal said. "Quick and sure. He took a straight razor and cut the victim's gullet with great force. He didn't bother to remove the weapon. I found it lying on the floor by the bed." Then he took out Bill Becker's ivory-handled razor, opened it dramatically, and laid it gently on the desk. There was dried blood on it.

The room was still. Jody and the judge were staring at the razor. The sheriff hadn't taken his eyes off the marshal. The marshal sat chewing magisterially. He folded up his notes and returned them to his shirt pocket.

"Is that your case?" the sheriff said. "What else have you got?"

The marshal looked smug. "Just a little quarrel between Harry Bewley and Bill Becker yesterday afternoon, in this very room, in front of several witnesses. There's real bad blood between them two. Seems Becker married Bewley's woman. I've got Bewley in custody. You can take him off to jail as you go."

The sheriff's eyes flashed briefly. "I've seen where you've got him." For the first time since the marshal had come in, the sheriff looked over at the judge. Their eyes were solemn. "I want to go up there," he said, "and I want you and the boy to come along."

"What in hell for?" the marshal bristled. "It's all been done."

"Come on," the sheriff said, his voice sharp. He had taken an envelope from his pocket and was sliding it under the razor. Deftly he shook it into the envelope without touching it.

"I ain't fed the animals yet," Jody blurted out. "They're hungry."

The sheriff's face softened. "Well, I guess Bill Becker can wait a few more minutes, but hurry."

Jody hurried. There wasn't much to feed them anyway, since the garbage run was incomplete. He tugged the fourth drum out of the truck, around the building, and into the pen where he quickly sorted and portioned out the food. He saved some moldy bread for the birds and animals in the grease pit. He didn't want to give them anything that smelled with Harry down there. Harry watched him break the bread in pieces and stuff some in each cage. He looked at the bread so directly that it occurred to Jody he must be hungry. But he couldn't give Harry what the animals ate.

"I'm sorry, Mr. Bewley," he said. He wasn't sure what all he was sorry for, but Harry simply nodded. On an impulse, Jody went to his pallet, picked up the sack with his toast and boiled eggs, and carried it down to the pit.

"I'd be obliged if you'd share my lunch, Mr. Bewley," he said hurriedly. "I can't eat all this anyway. Here's an egg for you and one for me, and we've got some bread." He quickly took an egg and a piece of toast and set the sack down by Harry's free hand. Then because he was embarrassed, he took a big bite from his cold toast and cracked his egg.

"Why, I can't do—" Tears filled Harry's eyes. He quietly opened the sack, took out a piece of toast, and broke it in half. He put one piece in his mouth, eyes closed. "That's good of you, son," he said in a husky voice. "I'm much obliged."

Jody brought the water bucket and they both took a long drink. Then he hurried around to fill the drinking troughs of the animals. By that time the sheriff was standing in the doorway.

"Let's go, son," he said, but his face was kindly, and his deep voice was soft as the church organ at communion time.

Chapter Five

"Get in," the sheriff said.

Jody opened the shiny door with the shield on it and climbed in. The sheriff got in the driver's side, started the car, and away they went, leaving the marshal to come in his truck.

"Tell me where to turn," the sheriff said.

Jody gave directions and they ripped through the little town in a few minutes. When they came to the house with the black Buick in front of it, there was a hearse turning into the drive. The sheriff touched his siren once, pulled up alongside it, and yelled at the driver.

"Wait here until I tell you to come up to the house."

He parked his car twenty yards from the house and took a camera from the glove compartment. "Come on," he said to Jody. Stay behind me and don't touch anything."

He took a picture of the front of the house. "Was that door closed when you came up this morning?"

"No sir. It was standing open. Or not standing exactly, kind of sagging, but opened out this way."

"So the marshal shut it," the Sheriff said.

"He shut it this morning too, when we come out. Had to lift up on it to get it to shut."

"Didn't you say you went back into the house?"

"Yes sir, but I went in the other door over there."

"It wasn't locked?"

"No. I opened it and walked in."

The sheriff was studying the broken door carefully. He took two pictures of it from close range. Then he took a handkerchief, lifted up carefully on the doorknob, and pulled the battered door open. "Tell me when it's about as far open as when you first saw it."

"Pretty wide," said Jody, "almost all the way. There. About there."

The Sheriff took two more pictures. Then he turned and took a close-up of the shattered doorjamb where the latch had torn out.

Carefully they stepped into the room. The sheriff looked steadily at the gaping slash in Bill's throat, at the arm sprawled out. More pictures: ones of the little washstand on the far side of the bed with the basin and all, of everything Jody had seen there last night, except the razor.

"Now," the sheriff said, "show me as near as you can where the razor was lying before that damn fool picked it up."

Jody pointed at the exact spot. The sheriff took a picture of him pointing at the floor. Inches from his hand the dead man pointed too.

"Never mind the other room for now. He's been rummaging around in there until there's nothing like it was. I may need you to go over that later."

They went back outside and carefully, obliquely, the sheriff worked his way around the house. The marshal was right. Jody's trail showed clearly in the tall weeds, with a second trail trampled by the marshal. The sheriff took two more pictures, then moved in to look more closely. Suddenly he stopped and bent over, studying the ground. It was a spot near the path to the toilet where the growth was greener and the earth was moist. It was obviously the place Rose Becker habitually poured the dishwater. Unlike the hard earth around, this spot was almost marshy. There, in the soft ground, was a print of a shoe.

The Sheriff looked at it a long time. Then he took a picture.

Nearby was the lean-to room, which Jody now saw was the kitchen, with a window near the corner. On the sill was a little piece of dried earth. The sheriff took a picture. Then he stood and looked at it meditatively while Jody fought back nausea. At last the sheriff raised his eyes to the sloping lean-to roof. Before him, almost at eye level, there was a smudge of dried mud on the shingles. He took another picture.

"All right," the sheriff said, "that'll do."

They went back around the house to the front. The sheriff sat down on the fender of the big Buick. Jody stood facing him, stirring the half-dead grass around the bare spot with his shoe.

"What work does Harry Bewley do? How does he make a living?" the sheriff asked.

"He don't work," Jody said. "He got all shot up inside in the war. He gets a pension." He stopped a bit, then felt he owed Harry a better defense. "At Christmas time he makes toys and little pretty things. Some people buy them."

The marshal's old truck was rattling up the long drive. It stopped beside the sheriff's car, and the marshal got out, slow. The sheriff waited patiently while the marshal seated himself in Bill Becker's old chair.

"Now, first, there wasn't any murderer," the sheriff said. "If there had been, it would have to be Rose Becker. I guess you've talked to Rose."

The marshal was looking blank. "No," he said at last. "I ain't yet."

"Well, you should have." The sheriff stood up. "Come over here," he said, and went to the door. "Take a good look at the latch. It's not locked. Did you unlock it?"

"No," said the marshal.

"Jody said the other door wasn't locked. Seems like the Beckers didn't lock their doors at night." He waited for the marshal to take that in. "That means an intruder wouldn't have to break a door to get in."

The marshal gawked at the latch.

"Now," said the sheriff, like a teacher in a classroom, "look at the door. It's broken from the inside. See here where the splinters all point outward? If you look at the door from the edge, you can see it bulge out in the middle." He pointed to the latch. "Here, where the latch broke out a piece of the jamb, see, it's splintered out on the outside."

The marshal sat flat down on the ground. He simply sank down slowly.

"Here's what happened. Rose Becker got up in the morning, wrapped the blanket around her, and went into Bill's room through the connecting door. There she saw Bill with his throat cut. What does she do? Goes into a panic. She tries to run out the door without opening it first, and busts it all to hell."

He turned to Jody. "Rose is a big, strong woman, right? and instead of running through an open door and smack into the Buick, she just crashed right through it. It's a pretty flimsy old door anyway."

"Who killed Becker?" the marshal said.

"Somebody inside the house," said the sheriff. "Unless someone else was in there, that means either Rose or Bill. If Rose didn't do it, which frankly doesn't look likely to me, it was a suicide."

The marshal stared. "But—my God, what a way to do yourself in!"

"Good as any, if you're in earnest about it, and the only way he could do it. He couldn't get up and hang himself, or take poison, or walk in front of a truck, but he could reach that razor. One quick deep slash," the sheriff took his right index finger and dragged it fast across his throat, "and that's all of it. He's done for before the razor hits the floor. If you want to look, you'll see blood on his right hand. He got the artery, gullet, and all, right down to the neckbone. Blood is everywhere."

The marshal fingered his badge while his face went through contortions. He hadn't given up yet, though. "What about the tracks around the house?"

"Well, now," said the sheriff, "that's a bit of a mystery. Somebody, not too large, tramped around in the back of the house. That person stepped in the only wet place in the whole yard and left a pretty good impression. It's a work shoe, been half-soled, probably a homemade repair job. It's not clean enough a cut to be the work of a shoe shop. If you find that shoe on Harry Bewley or in his house, you can put him behind the Beckers' house. But it doesn't make any difference. Whoever that was, Harry or not Harry, did a funny thing. He, or she, climbed up on a window sill and up onto the roof of the kitchen. I don't know what for, maybe to hide, but there's no sign that person was in the house. Even if he was, he didn't smear Bill Becker's hand in his own blood."

The marshal's head bent forward. The sheriff sat still, waiting for it all to soak in.

"I ain't never seen Harry wear a shoe like that," the marshal said, finally.

"Tell you what I'd do, if I were you," the sheriff said, almost kindly. "I'd go back to that grease pit and let Mr. Bewley go. I'd be real respectful and considerate towards him. If you had to testify in a trial of Harry Bewley for murder of Bill Becker, your evidence would come all apart like a two–bit suitcase. Then, I reckon the defense attorney, probably a retired judge named Hanks, would likely ask you some questions that would be real embarrassing to you and to the profession of lawman."

The marshal finally raised his head and looked away into the fields on the horizon. He seemed to study them abstractly, as though searching for some distant landmark. Without looking at either of the others, he rose and trudged off. The truck started up and lumbered out of the yard.

The sheriff waved to the hearse, and the driver, who had been waiting in the road all this while, backed up the drive quickly. The two men opened the back of the hearse and lugged Bill Becker clumsily out the door, wrapped up in the bedclothes, his guilty right hand still flung out stiffly toward Jody, like a gesture, an appeal, for understanding. They folded and stuffed him into the hearse, sweating and panting in the blistering heat of late morning..

"You better ask the coroner to take a look," the sheriff told the driver, "but you can tell him I don't expect him to find anything new. Tell him I'll be along in half an hour."

The hearse rolled softly down the drive, out onto the road, and slipped out of earshot.

"Now, Jody," the sheriff said, "let me see that left shoe."

The sheriff's voice came to him strangely, as if from a great distance. Suddenly he felt very weak. There was a tingling in his face and scalp. He was getting sick. He felt chilled in the bright hot sun, and a cold sweat came to his forehead. Not able to stand, he sank down on the ground and leaned back against the wall of the house.

The sheriff waited, watching him closely.

Slowly Jody began to be less dizzy and faint. His eyes filled with tears. He leaned over and started to remove his shoe.

"Never mind," the sheriff said. "I can see the dirt caked in the instep from here. We don't have to carry it around the house and match it with the impression, do we?"

"No."

"Why don't you tell me what that was all about?" the sheriff said, kindly, but the black eyes were boring into him.

So Jody told him everything. At first he was almost too abashed to talk, but gradually he let it fall free from him, more and more willingly. "I don't know why," he said after he had told his story. "I didn't even know I was going to do it. Seemed like I had to know how it was with Bill and Rose. If they had been there at the first, maybe I would have asked them, if they seemed friendly. I mean, asked them how they got along with all them problems they had. How they stayed with it, what they did about—about sex, and all. Seemed like if I knowed I would be easier in my mind, and knowed what I might of had to do in a like case."

"I see," the sheriff said. That was all. He didn't laugh at him, or scold or shame him.

"Am I goin' to jail?" Jody asked. I guess I can stand it if I have to, he thought.

The sheriff didn't say anything for a minute. He didn't smile or frown or give any sign. "Well, now," he said at last, "first, someone has to press charges. That would be the owners of the property. Now Bill Becker won't press charges. I don't know yet what Mrs. Becker might want to do."

Jody made himself look the sheriff straight in the eyes. "Are you going to tell her?"

The sheriff didn't blink. "You see," he said, "Mrs. Becker has had a bad time. Seems to me there's no call for anybody to worry her about this thing right now. But you see, she's been done a wrong. Some time or other, when it won't hurt quite so bad, she ought to know about that. Then she could decide whether she should press charges or not."

"So you are going to tell her."

"Well, now," the sheriff said, "I'll confess that I'd rather not. I think I'll have to brood on it a little while before I say what I would do. Maybe I could feel all right about it if I simply let all this be forgot." He watched Jody's face closely. "But I thought maybe you might want to tell her."

Jody swallowed hard. He could feel a blush go up his neck and cheeks, until his whole face felt hot. He couldn't think of anything to say.

"Well, anyway," said the sheriff, "we won't either of us do anything about this for right now. Let's put old Bill Becker decently in the ground and give the lady a few days to heal a little. Come on. I'll take you back to the marshal's."

They got in the car and started back. Jody turned the conversation over and over in his mind, all the way back. At last, nearing the store, he turned to the sheriff and said, "Thank you."

"Sure," the sheriff said. He pulled up by the store, where only yesterday Rose had parked the Buick and carried Bill inside. He looked at Jody and said quietly, "You're a good man, Jody Carpenter."

Jody bowed his head and didn't try to speak. Slowly he opened the door, got out, and looked back at the sheriff. The sheriff touched his hat, put the car in gear, and drove away.

Chapter Six

Even the Animal Store seemed to reflect the strangeness of the day. The marshal's truck was nowhere around, and the store was quiet. The stove sat with the chairs and crates around it, as though it had called a session, but no one was there. Through the door open to the garage, he heard the judge and Harry talking quietly. He went on through the office and joined them. Harry sat on the floor of the pit where he had been since morning. The judge sat on the garage floor, his feet dangling over the edge of the pit. Jody sat down on the other side of the pit, facing the judge, hanging his feet over the edge too. Harry leaned back against the wire cages and looked up at them.

"Well, son, let's have the bad news," Harry said. "Are they gonna haul me off somewheres and try me?"

"The sheriff says it was a suicide," Jody said. "He told the marshal he ought to let you go."

The judge's face bloomed in a grin. Harry took a deep breath and blew it out through his puckered lips in a long sigh. "Well! In that case, possum old buddy," he winked at the solemn animal in the cage near his head, "looks like I might get out of here afore you. I'll send you a cake with some wire snips in it. That's my buddy," he said to Jody. "He says he wouldn't mind getting a parole hisself. You got any idea when the marshal might come by and let me go?"

"I dunno," Jody said. "Me and the sheriff stayed until the hearse took Mr. Becker away. The marshal went somewheres. I don't know where, except maybe to talk to Mrs. Becker."

Harry's face turned dark. "What's he bothering her fer? Stupid shithead! Don't he know she needs to be left alone?" He got up on his knees and yanked at the cuffs on his arm. All the cages in the pit shook as he jerked at the handcuffs; the birds fluttered and squawked and the possum paced his cage hurriedly. Two young squirrels were racing around wildly. Harry gave their cage a kick.

"Hey, hold on!" the judge said. "You're going to hurt yourself or hurt the animals. Now, Rose isn't exactly a helpless child, even if she is in a state about Bill. If the marshal gets smart, she might just break his nose. So settle down. She'll be all right."

Harry stopped thrashing around and slowly sat back down on the floor as the squawking and fluttering began to subside. "Yeah," he grinned, "she might just do that. Serve him right, the shithead."

They all laughed at that, forcing it a little. Then they got quiet. Harry told some stories about the old times with Bill and Rose, including the one about the twenty-dollar fine, and made the judge say it was so. Neither the judge nor Jody let on that the story had been told before. Finally he asked Jody to tell him all about how Bill died. Jody told everything as gently as he could, except he didn't tell anything about the previous night or his talk with the Sheriff about it. The two men listened soberly. Harry's pale blue eyes were misty, and the old sick look seemed engraved around his mouth. When Jody had finished his account, they all sat in silence for some minutes.

"Well, he was a good friend," said Harry at last, "and I don't care what nobody else says." His voice was husky, full of pain. "I reckon he did hisself in, all right. The poor old son of a bitch. You ought'n of done it, old Bill." He gripped the cage, as though he meant to give it another shake, but when he lifted his face and looked squarely into the sad eyes of the possum he relaxed his grip and wept softly. "You know what I'm gonna do?" he said to the judge. "If Rose'll let me, I'm gonna save up enough money to buy Bill a headstone. Bill ought to have a stone."

Doc came through the door, wiping his balding head with a huge handkerchief. He stopped abruptly at the scene before him, of Harry in the pit with the judge and Jody perched on the edges. Then he came into the end of the pit where the steps came up and sat down on the top step facing Harry.

"She's all right," he told Harry. "She had her a good long cry, and Ella Gamble got her to eat a little. She's strong as a horse, and she's sensible. She wants to talk to you, Judge, about the funeral and all. We were doing fine until the marshal showed up. He asked her a lot of questions, made her tell the story all over two or three times. He told her a yarn about how somebody had been prowling around the house, and got her all upset about that. Then he asked her if she didn't have a lover hanging around, and that made her mad. She told him to kiss her ass and go to hell." Doc grinned wide. "He didn't do that, but he left anyway."

The judge pulled his legs back out of the pit and lumbered stiffly to his feet. "I'll go up there and talk to her. It sounds like the marshal hasn't given up on you, Harry. Now don't give him any sass. He can't keep you here long." He hitched his trousers up over his paunch and lumbered out.

Harry and Doc and Jody sat on the cool, oily concrete floor and talked about Rose and how she would live now, and how hard it would be without Bill. The afternoon wore on. After about an hour Doc reminded himself that he had some sick folks to see, got to his feet, and walked out through the office door. He had a dirty smudge on the seat of his trousers.

"I wish I could go see Rose," Harry said. "I wish I could help her a little. The marshal ought not to bother her with all that crap." There was a flash of anger in his voice. "The marshal ain't real smart." He was silent for a minute. Then he spoke again, more calmly. "No, that ain't the problem. He's smart enough. He just don't know nothing about people." He looked squarely at Jody. "Do you think I could of killed Bill Becker?"

"No," Jody said.

Harry nodded. "Well, I had to kill some people in the war. But I couldn't never kill nobody just because I was mad about something, or because I'd been wronged. And as fer Bill Becker, I couldn't of killed him even to keep him from killing me." He raised his face to stare into the possum's somber eyes. "You know, I wouldn't be any good at killing even in war, now." He looked at his shackled hand, musing.

In a minute he looked up. "I guess the marshal couldn't know about all that. But as fer Rose, now," his voice got trembly, "a person wouldn't have to know much to understand Rose. She's a good woman that's had to go through too much, and folks ought not trouble her in her grief. Even the marshal ought to know that whatever happened to Bill it ain't Rose's fault."

Watching him snubbed up there against the chicken wire, Jody suddenly had a flash of Bill Becker's face in Rose's arms, Rose rocking him against her breasts, and Bill's hand reaching up to touch her cheek. A sharp pain went through Jody's abdomen. He felt he was peering into Harry's anguish through a crack in his soul. The sensation troubled him. Self–conscious, shuffling his feet, he felt called on to say something. "She sure is a pretty lady."

Harry looked up at him with a start. For a second Jody thought Harry might swear at him. It was like somebody had slapped him on the back too hard, and he didn't know whether to hit back or return a greeting. Then he broke into a high, cackling laugh.

"Why, hell, boy! She ain't no such thing. Rose pretty! She's homely as a mud pie."

He had a good hard laugh, while Jody slowly turned scarlet. Then there was an awkward time while Harry's laughter settled into intermittent, self–conscious bursts, then stopped altogether, as he first noticed, then grasped, Jody's confusion.

"I'm sorry, Jody," he said. "I didn't mean to laugh at you. It's just that the idea is so—well, I guess I know what you mean to say. She wasn't too bad–looking, once on a time. But honest, son, she ain't pretty. You gotta understand me. There ain't a face on earth I'd rather—" He stopped a moment. He and Jody looked each other full in the eyes. "Well, I guess you've figgered it out. I guess you see right through all of it, and you know I love that old horse of a woman." He laughed shortly. "Love her more'n myself." Something turned loose in his pain–drawn face. He looked down at the gray, hard floor with a smile. "When you really love somebody," he said, "it don't make no difference what she looks like."

A sense of the unreal began to steal over Jody. It was like the floor under him had suddenly fallen away, and he was looking down on the pit full of animals, and Harry, from a great height. At the same time, he was still there. The sober possum turned at that moment and looked Jody full in the eyes. He turned apprehensively, and sure enough the barred owl was looking straight at him too. He felt like he was floating, he couldn't feel his arms or legs at all, and he wasn't sure he could make his body stand up. Troubled, he rose numbly, took the water bucket to the pump, and filled it. The sounds of the creaking pump and the water spurting into the bucket, into itself, came clear and sharp, as though he had never heard them before. He went around to all the pens, pouring fresh water for the animals and birds. It seemed that all of them looked at him knowingly. Even as the sensation was beginning to wear off in the stench and heat of the sordid pens, he came to Rupe's pen at last, and stooping down to pour his drink, he raised his face to see Rupe's brown eyes staring quietly into his own. Surely, surely, Rupe understood it all.

The marshal's truck finally showed up about four o'clock. Jody was out in the lot when he heard it pull in. He had just finished burying the contents of the coffee can the marshal had given Harry to relieve himself in and was rinsing it out. He brought the can back to the pit where Harry was dozing fitfully and set it down as unobtrusively as he could near Harry's knee. As he climbed out of the pit he heard the marshal and Johnny talking in the office.

"No luck at all," Johnny said. "I been hanging round that cafe all afternoon, just like you said, watching fer a work shoe with a homemade half–sole. The only one I seen was on Ben Fenderson, and he ain't exactly a little man, unless you call two hunnert and thirty pounds little."

"No," the marshal said. He sounded sullen.

"Well, you know, this here might take awhile. I'd like to help you out, Marshal, but I don't see making a career out of something that won't get you nowheres. Supposing you find this Romeo, what then?"

"It's all part of the investigation," the marshal said doggedly. "I got to fit it all in together afore I'll know what's what. Maybe Rose had a boyfriend she let in the house and he killed Bill. Maybe Harry killed Bill, and all them tracks and somebody climbing up on a roof is just something he set up to make it look all confused."

"Well," Johnny said, "I'll keep looking. I'm kind of curious about who's been slipping into Rose's bedroom anyway." Her gave a snort and a cackle. "Hey, that 'minds me. Did you ever hear the one about the traveling salesman's wife that had run up a big bill with the iceman?"

"Hey!" Harry yelled, behind Jody's back, and made him jump where he was listening at the door. "Marshal, damn it, come let me loose from this fucking cage."

Jody backed off into a corner and sat down on the floor, tucking his shoes under his legs as best he could. There was a scrape of the marshal's chair. He slowly came through the door and impassively looked down on Harry. Behind him Johnny leaned on the door frame.

"I ain't ready to turn you loose yet."

Harry's eyes flashed. "Well, I'm sure as hell ready to get loose. Just because you got a dime–store badge, that ain't enough reason to keep a man in a sty like this."

"You're my number–one suspect, and you ain't going loose until I get my investigation done. I seen it with my own eyes, how you and Bill had bad blood atween you, and I know Rose was your girl—"

"You don't know nothing about it!" Harry was shouting now. "You've got shit fer brains, and I'll tell you what else, you're gonna let me go or I'm gonna come out of here dragging this whole zoo with me, and stomp your ass."

The marshal let the echoes from the concrete pit die out. Then he drew his gun slowly. "Air you threaten' me?"

Johnny stirred uneasily. "Hey, Marshal," he said mildly.

"Let me in, John," said a voice behind him. The judge pushed his way into the garage. He shot a quick frown at Harry and walked up to the marshal slowly. "Now, Marshal, let me remind you that your prisoner either has to be formally charged or let go. Since you don't have a proper facility to house him or feed him, you'll have to book him into the county jail if you're going to charge him."

The marshal chewed deliberately as if pondering a great mystery. At last he spat on the floor and put his gun away. "Now I'll tell you something, Judge. I tried to give him to Sheriff Yates, and he didn't see fit to take him. The kindly citizens of Trasherdell ain't furnished me no shiny patrol car with a purty red spotlight, and I'm sure as hell not going to drive my own vee–hickle, at my own expense, to take this suspect to Ashton."

There was an uncomfortable silence. Jody struggled with an impulse to rise, take off his shoe, and present it to the marshal, but he sat in his corner, chewing the forefinger of his right hand. Suddenly Harry laid back his head, turned his face toward the possum, and began to laugh. He started laughing low, then just let it rip, with the hard walls of the garage throwing echoes everywhere. Everyone watched him for a few seconds. Then Johnny began to laugh also, his baritone blending antiphonally with Harry's shrill tenor. Pretty soon the judge chimed in, and then finally the marshal, slow and heavy, like a viol in a four–part fugue.

"Oh, what the hell!" Harry said at last, wiping his eyes with his free hand, his face relaxed into a big grin. "We can take my vee–

hickle, if you ain't too proud to drive it. Or you can shackle me to the steering column, and I'll drive you, yore marshalship. Sorry I ain't got no purty red light either."

"Well then, I guess that's settled," said the judge promptly, "and so we can get on with business. Marshal, if you'll release your prisoner into my custody, I'll see he gets fed and so relieve the City of Trasherdell of that expense. I'll have him back here in two hours, ready to be delivered to Ashton. If you like, I'll call the sheriff and let him know you're coming."

The marshal stood, undecided, chewing his tobacco slowly. Finally he said, "I'll call the sheriff myself!" in an assertive tone. He took a key from his pocket, went down into the pit, and took the handcuffs off Harry's wrist. Harry stood up stiffly and began hobbling up the steps, the marshal following him.

"Six o'clock," the marshal said.

"We'll be here," the judge said. "Come on, Harry. Rose wants to talk to you and to Jody, too. I stopped by the cafe and asked Art to set up the back room for the four of us. We'll go by my place so you men can clean up."

Jody grabbed his bundle with his change of clothes and was out of the garage quickly. He didn't want Johnny or the marshal to have any longer than necessary to notice his shoes. The judge and Harry followed him out. Once away from the store, they chuckled softly to one another. Harry clapped the judge on the shoulder and said, "I owe you one, old man."

Chapter Seven

They got into the judge's big black DeSoto and drove the two blocks to his rambling white frame house with its pillars all along the cool front porch and climbing rose on the trellis. There for the first time in his life Jody took a bath in a long white tub he could stretch out in with hot and cold water coming right out of the faucet and soap that left him smelling like honeysuckle, and thick towels to dry on half as big as a blanket. Jody put on his clean clothes and combed his hair in front of the full–length mirror. As he gathered up his soiled clothes, he was suddenly aware they were dirty and smelled of sweat and the animals and the garbage. He wanted to stop and think about that, about why he had seldom noticed the smells before, why he felt ashamed, but the judge was in a hurry, so he stuffed them into his sack and wadded it up tightly. While Harry was cleaning up, he walked back to the store and threw the sack-full of clothing into the pen by the back door.

Back at the house, he saw Harry come out the screen door, stuffing one of the judge's white shirts into his trousers, freshly shaved and hair slicked down. The shirt was baggy on Harry, and he had to roll up the sleeves. Still, he looked nicer than Jody had ever seen him, with his dark thin face and black hair rich–textured against the open– necked white shirt.

The judge didn't stop to lock the house. They drove to Mrs. Gamble's house, and there was Rose sitting on the front porch with Mrs. Gamble waiting for them. She had on the same dress Jody had got for her that morning. Mrs. Gamble must have loaned her some underclothes that must have been too small, but anyway she looked decent where the dress gapped open in front, and she had some stockings on too. Her cheeks were red–splotched and her eyes were

In Earthen Vessels

bleared and sunken, but her face was calm. She even tried to smile at them as they got out from the car.

Mrs. Gamble patted Rose's arm and said she'd be waiting up for her. She insisted that Rose would stay with her for a night or two, or as long as she wanted. Rose hugged her and said she was a dear friend.

Harry said huskily, "I'm so sorry, Rose." They hugged one another, and Rose cried a little on Harry's borrowed shirt. Then she gave the judge's arm a squeeze. Finally she laid her hand, soft and tentative, on Jody's shoulder, and her mouth said thank you though no sound came out. Jody couldn't say anything back, but he managed, shy as he was, to pat her hand on his shoulder. They said good–bye to Mrs. Gamble. Harry and Rose got in the back seat of the DeSoto. Jody sat up front with the judge, and away they went.

In the back room of Art's Cafe there was a square table set with a white cloth. Art's pretty daughter Sally brought them a huge steaming bowl of mashed potatoes and a platter full of chicken–fried steaks. There was rich cream gravy, green beans cooked with ham scraps, and a whole loaf of store–bought white bread on a tray. Rose said she didn't think she could eat, but under Harry's coaxing she took some small portions. As Harry and the judge kept up a patter of light talk she began to taste things and little by little surrendered to her appetite and ate heartily. As for Jody, no grief or shyness could have overridden his craving. His daily bread had been the scant, nauseous food the marshal and his stingy wife supplied; like the animals in his care, he ate without enjoyment, because he had to. Now, the hot rich steak and gravy and the bread as sweet and soft as cake were like the benison of God. He abandoned himself to the meal as a weary child takes sleep.

"Now, Rose," the judge said, "I'll be with you in the funeral home. Anything you don't understand, you ask me, okay? Harry's got to go to the sheriff's office with the marshal, but I'm sure Lonnie will let him go with us. We're all going to be with you all the time. Whatever help you need—"

Rose laid down her fork, her eyes watering. She snorted back a sob, propped her elbows on either side of her plate, and looked the judge straight in the face. "Now, Judge," she said steadily, "let's get one thing straight. I'm gonna manage. I don't reckon I'll ever be all right again, but I ain't gonna lie down and die." She stopped abruptly, swallowed hard, and went on. "You're my dear friend. I do need your help, and I'm grateful for everything, but it's awful important to me to take care of my old Bill myself, any way I can."

"Sure, Rose," the judge said softly, "I understand."

Rose leaned back in her chair and took her arms off the table. It rocked back toward Jody slightly. "What I aim to do," she said, "is sell Bill's car. Surely that'll buy him a coffin and a little scrap of ground to put it in."

"Sell Bill's car?" said Harry, his eyes big in his thin face.

Under the table Jody felt a slight motion as the judge gave Harry a sharp kick.

"If that ain't enough," Rose said, "I'll see what I can borry on the old house."

"But, Rose," said Harry gently, "how are you gonna live?"

"I don't know, Harry," she said. "There's time enough to worry about that when I've done what I can fer Bill."

Harry lowered his eyes to his plate and self-consciously took another forkful of mashed potatoes.

"There's something else," Rose said, her voice husky. "Last night, before Bill—before he went to sleep—" She paused, bowed her head a second, then looked back up at Harry. "He asked me to do something for him. He said the next time I seen you, Harry—that—that I should tell you he was sorry fer what happened atween you two yesterday." The tears were coming freely now, but her voice was steady.

"And he said he knowed you was our friend and only wished us good, and he hoped you'd forgive him."

She bowed her head and wept quietly. There was a strange sound from Harry's throat. Then she looked up at Jody, who was watching her with a panic of anticipation.

"And Jody, he said you was a good boy and he was sorry to have spoke harsh to you."

They were all watching her in stone silence. Suddenly she broke completely and began to sob. She stood up, waved off Harry, who was getting out of his chair, and hurried off to the door where the rest rooms were.

Harry, Jody, and the judge sat quietly for a moment. Then Harry said to the judge, "Afore she comes back there's something you've got to know. Jody, this has got to be kept quiet, do you understand?"

He waited for Jody to nod, then went on. "Right next to the gas tank on Bill's Buick, bolted onto the frame on the left side, there's a metal box. You got to get it off afore she sells that car. They is two thousand dollars in it."

After a long silence, the judge sucked in his breath. "Left side, you say?"

Harry nodded.

"But, Harry," Jody said, as soon as he found his voice, "why not just tell her it's there, so she wouldn't have to sell that car?"

"I almost did, but that would of been a mistake. You see, my young friend, it would take away."

"Take away?"

Harry nodded, slowly, his eyes on Jody. "They ain't much a person can do fer the dead, but Rose needs to do something fer Bill real bad, something that costs her, don't you see?" He waited a moment for the point to sink in. "Now when the time is right, we'll find a way to get Rose that money. She can even buy back the car, if she wants. But once she's sold it, she'll always know she made a sacrifice fer her old Bill."

Rose came back through the door at the end of the room. Harry brushed his finger across his lips.

"Come on, Harry," the judge said, rising. "We've got to take you back to the marshal. I'll be by the sheriff's office in a little while."

They all went with the judge and waited, silent, while he paid Art for the meal. Then there was a short ride to the marshal's place, where the marshal was already standing beside Harry's truck. He had the handcuffs ready. He was going to take Harry up on his offer to the letter.

Harry got in the driver's side. The marshal cuffed him to the steering column and slammed his door.

"You was almost late," the marshal said.

"Put it on my bill," the judge said.

The marshal snorted, walked around to the other side of the truck, and got in. Harry waved at them with a rueful grin and drove away.

The sight of the marshal putting handcuffs on Harry was clearly bothering Rose. She fidgeted as the truck drove off. "Judge—" she said tentatively.

"Don't you worry about Harry, Rose," the judge said. "We're going to get him out of that fix. There's no way the marshal can keep him under arrest."

Slowly Jody started to get out. For the first time, he really hated the idea of going to his smelly pallet in the marshal's store. But the judge reached over and put his hand on his arm.

"Come along with us, son," he said. "We might need you."

Jody hesitated only a moment. "I'll need to fetch the animals clean water," he said. The judge nodded. Jody hurried through the store to the pens and began pumping fresh water into his bucket. As he made the rounds hurriedly, speaking to all the animals, he remembered with a pang they hadn't had much to eat today. With his own belly pleasantly full, he had a rush of guilt. "I'm sorry," he told Rupe as he tossed out the filmy, hot water from the pan and refilled it. Rupe gave him a single wag from his tail. Finished, he propped open the back door with the board and padlocked the front door.

Rose was sitting up front with the judge, so Jody got in the back seat of the DeSoto. Once out of Trasherdell, the judge spurred the big car up to sixty, and within a few miles they overtook and passed Harry's truck. They all waved as the DeSoto sailed by. Jody had never gone this fast in his life. The judge was keeping up a steady patter, coaxing Rose to talk. Jody quit trying to listen to what they were saying. He watched the telephone poles flash by and listened to the drone of the engine and felt the vibrations in his feet and buttocks and suddenly felt very tired.

He closed his eyes and was aware that he had to sleep. He saw visions of the animals in their cages, all looking at him knowingly. Rupe and the possum and the big owl and Nellie and Harry were there in cages around him. Yes, there was Bill Becker in his cage too, saying something Jody couldn't understand. When he tried to get up and go closer to hear, he found that he was in a chicken–wire cage himself, and Sally was bringing him fresh water in an earthenware bowl.

Chapter Eight

The jolt of the car stopping woke him. He dragged his consciousness up from the bottom of some deep lake as the engine shut off and the vibrations all stopped. He was sprawled on the back seat with his head against the car door. Before he could move, he heard Rose talking quietly to the judge.

"Let him sleep a little, the poor feller. He's been through a long day. You wouldn't believe how gentle and caring he was to me this morning, Judge, like a mammy tending her baby. Whaddaya s'pose it is makes some kids that way, and some so mean?"

"Hard to tell for certain," the judge said. "But for one thing, I'd say that Josh and Mary Carpenter put a lot of love into his making."

"Yeah. Guess that's about all they had to put in."

The judge chuckled lightly. "A lot of love, prayers, wild greens, mashed potatoes, and a twelve–hour work day. Funny what you can do with the least materials if you really try."

"I reckon so," Rose said. "But then take me. My old Pa got fired from his work in Arkansaw 'cause he was drinking on the job, so him and Ma and me started fer California. Well, we got to Trasherdell, and they was arguing about some money Pa thought Ma had hid back. They got into a big fight in the middle of the street, and I just walked off so's I wouldn't have to listen to what they called each other. I sat around behind the schoolhouse and bawled fer about an hour. When I went back they was gone. I was fifteen.

"I just sat down outside Art's cafe and waited fer them, but they never come back. Long about dark, Bill and Harry pulled up and went into the cafe to eat. I was still there when they come out. They looked at me, and then they come over. Harry said, 'What's the matter, Darlin, has somebody forgot you?' I started bawlin like a fool. Harry and Bill looked at one another. Bill said, 'Harry, we forgot that pie we was gonna have. Let's go back and have some of Art's pecan pie. Won't you come join us, ma'am, while you wait, and have a cup and a bite to keep us company?'

"So they took me into Art's and fed me and let me talk. I blubbered it all out. Harry said, 'You come and stay with us tonight. You can have my bed, and I'll double up with Bill. Then tomorra likely your folks will be back.' I went with Bill and Harry, and of course my folks never came back. They took me to Widow Gamble's the next day, and I growed up there. That was sixteen year ago, and I ain't seen Pa nor Ma since, don't know where they is."

Jody heard the truck pulling up beside them. "There's Harry and the marshal," the judge said. "Wake up, Jody."

Jody sat up and rubbed his eyes. They were parked on the side of the courthouse. The sun was still shining on the big clock in the dome, but a light was on over a basement door in the south wall. They all got out. The marshal walked around the truck. He took the handcuff from the steering column and snapped it on his own wrist.

They all went up the walk together, all conversation snuffed out by the fact of the handcuffs. The marshal pulled Harry firmly along, opened the frosted-glass door, and pushed him inside. At a huge cluttered desk Sheriff Yates sat with his feet propped up, sipping a cup of coffee and thumbing through rumpled forms on a clipboard. The sheriff took them all in with a glance.

"I brought you something," the marshal said and turned to take the handcuffs from Harry's wrist.

"Sit down, Harry," the sheriff said. He handed the marshal a printed form and a pen without comment. Harry sank into a seat across from the sheriff. The marshal set to work on the form with dogged concentration. Everyone else stood around. In the silence, the sheriff sipped his coffee deliberately.

"Guess that does it," the marshal said, tossing the paper and pen at the sheriff. "Now I'll be gettin' back." He looked at Jody a moment. "Don't forget we got work to do in the morning. I hope I won't catch you sleeping in again."

"You mean you're just taking my truck and leaving me here?" Harry asked.

"It was your idea," the marshal said with a grin. He gave a tip of his hat brim to nobody in particular and walked out, the shadow of the grin still on his face.

Rose sat down on the bench against the wall and began to cry softly.

"Would you like a cup of coffee, Mrs. Becker?" the sheriff asked.

"No," Rose said miserably.

The sheriff laid down his clipboard and picked up the paper the marshal had filled out. He looked at the judge and motioned toward the door with his head.

"Come on, Rose," the judge said. "The sheriff will need to talk to Harry a few minutes. Let's wait outside until he's finished."

Rose stood up slowly and let the judge guide her outside. When they were gone, the sheriff stood, looked at Harry for a long moment, and dropped the paper on his desk.

"Seems this form isn't quite properly filled out," he said. "That means I don't really have any grounds to hold you." He took a long sip of coffee.

"You mean I'm free?"

"After a manner of speaking. Of course, maybe you don't really want to be free."

"What?" Harry said with a snort.

"Look at it this way. Your dutiful marshal has got an idea in his head, and he's determined to play lawman. Now as soon as he turns his case over to the county attorney, if he does, he's going to be told that the county doesn't have enough evidence to prosecute you for killing Bill Becker." He stopped and looked Harry squarely in the face. "You didn't kill Bill Becker, did you?"

"Hell, Lonnie, you know I didn't."

"Well, then, suppose the marshal finally gets it through his head that you didn't, but he still won't accept the idea of suicide because to his thinking a murder is more interesting. Where does he go next?"

"What air you driving at?"

"He goes looking for another suspect," the sheriff said. Harry's head jerked erect. "And the best suspect he has is Rose Becker."

"That's crazy!" Harry said.

The sheriff said nothing, just stood looking out his window, cradling his coffee cup.

Harry stood up, looked over at Jody, looked down at his hands. "Well," he said at last, "that's a nuisance Rose don't need right now. Reckon it's better if I go on being his suspect fer a while."

Without looking at Harry, the sheriff nodded his head abstractedly.

"So air you gonna lock me up?"

"I could, I guess," the sheriff said, "but then again, I don't have to. The form being improperly completed, you see. I could just send you back to Trasherdell in the judge's custody."

"And let the marshal pen me up with his other livestock?" Harry said angrily.

"It's up to you," the sheriff said. "Of course, if you stay here, the county attorney's office has to decide, forthwith, as the law says, whether you should be charged. On the other hand, if you were in Trasherdell, you could help the marshal get on with his investigation. It would be handy for him to question you whenever he needed to question somebody."

Harry stared at the sheriff's back for a moment. Then he sank down in his chair with a groan. "Oh shit! How long do we have to put up with all this?"

"Not long," the sheriff said, turning around. "I'd just as soon not put Rose through an inquest, but if that has to happen, that should be the end of the case. My guess is, the marshal will get tired and drop it all before that's necessary."

"So what now?" Harry said. "He's gone with my truck."

"You are released into Mr. Hanks' custody. He will see that you're returned to Trasherdell. Now, I think you men ought to take Rose over to the funeral parlor and help her get through the arrangements."

Harry nodded. "Thanks, Lonnie."

"For old time's sake," the sheriff said.

Harry got up and motioned to Jody. As they were at the door, the sheriff stopped them. "One more thing, Harry. You've got to understand something. If anybody murdered Bill Becker, it had to be Rose."

"You don't think she did?" Harry said.

"Of course not. I'm just telling you to be alert. Don't let the marshal get hold of that idea." He walked over and clapped Jody on the shoulder. "You be a good jailer, now. You keep everything quiet and orderly, all right?" The fingers on his shoulder gave a gentle pressure, like a signal.

Two blocks west of the courthouse the judge pulled to a stop beside the Matthias Funeral Parlor. It was a big white stucco building with two columns flanking the front door and stained–glass windows on the south side. They sat in the car and looked at the front of the building, nobody eager to get out. Through the door came an elderly farm woman leaning on a young man's arm. Her face was drawn up in surprised pain, and she had a red handkerchief held in her knotty bronze hand. The man had on a heavy brown suit and walked clumsily in his new shoes. Every patch of him that stuck out of his clothes was sun–reddened, right to the roots of his blond hair. The woman stared back at Jody with the same look he had seen in the eyes of the wild animals in their cages. Suddenly, she spit at him.

"Come on, Mama," the son said, "leave alone. It ain't their fault."

He steered her down the street toward a dust–stained Model A.

"Oh God," Rose said. She began to sob. Beside her Harry put his arm around her shoulders.

"You wait here a minute, Rose. I'll see if Matthias can talk to us now," the judge said. "Come on, Jody."

They left Harry comforting Rose and stepped into the gloomy interior of the white building. There was a thick green carpet and a lavender–colored sofa in the waiting room. A casket stood open on the right in an alcove. On the little stand in front of it a book was opened up. On the left was a massive mahogany desk with two chairs drawn up in front of it. Behind it sat a man in a black suit, writing.

The judge said, "Good evening, Mr. Matthias."

The man in the suit looked up and nodded. He had black hair slicked down on both sides, with a pronounced gray streak over each temple, a very long chin, and long exquisite hands with a diamond ring that glittered in the light of his desk lamp as he laid down his pen.

"Good evening, Mr. Hanks," he said, taking Jody in with a glance of distaste. "Sit down."

The judge sat down in one of the chairs, and Jody, with some reluctance, sat in the other. It wasn't at all clear whether he was welcome. Mr. Matthias ignored him totally.

"You're here about Mr. Becker, I presume."

"Yes," the judge said. "Mrs. Becker is outside."

"Umm, yes. Well, what's to do, Mr. Hanks? The Beckers don't have a burial policy with us. They don't have a burial lot. I suspect they don't have any money. I doubt she can afford a funeral."

The judge shifted slightly in his chair. "I have come to see that you conclude that she can."

Mr. Matthias smiled a little. "Does that mean you intend to pay for it?"

"Not necessarily. Mrs. Becker has some, uh, assets."

Mr. Matthias raised his eyebrows slightly.

"She has a car, a Buick sedan, in very good condition," the judge said.

"I am not in need of a Buick sedan, regardless of condition."

"Give her credit on it," the judge said amiably. "Give her a week or two to dispose of it."

"My dear Mr. Hanks," said Mr. Matthias, leaning back in his chair, "why should I? Who is Mrs. Becker? Who was Mr. Becker? A cripple, a former convict, and a suicide, or so it would appear."

The judge stared at Mr. Matthias. Mr. Matthias stared resolutely back.

"I would think," said the judge at last, "that death, and burial, should be available to everyone."

His voice was precise, charged with restrained feeling. Jody had never heard him speak like that.

"Oh come, let's be frank, shall we? You are an intelligent, an educated man. I run a business, not a welfare agency. For a fee I provide some rather nauseous services, a casket, a small plot of earth, perhaps a stone—all of which, taken together, comprise my real trade, solace. I sell solace, that is to say, relief from guilt through an ultimate gesture of notice. When I am paid, I provide solace efficiently and with flair. But when I am not paid, I have little recourse." He paused to emphasize his point. "Now what would I do, if Mrs. Becker will not or cannot pay me? Shall I sue an indigent? That would be small profit. Shall I give her back Mr. Becker's remains and repossess the casket and the burial plot? I think not."

"Now, just a minute—"

"I'll tell you, Mr. Hanks, what I most dislike about all this." Mr. Matthias stood up from his desk. "My family has been in this business since before statehood. In the cemetery I administer are forty-two veterans of the Civil War, including my own grandfather, a recipient of the Medal of Honor. There are also a host of other godly and significant men. I do not relish burying a suicide among them. There was a time, sir, when it would not have been countenanced!"

He walked around the desk and stood, a very tall man, towering over them. "Who wants to be buried beside such a person? Who wants to bury a loved one beside him? If I put him among existing graves, there will perhaps be a protest. If I put him along the border perhaps I can never sell the adjacent plot, nor would I relish doing so. It is a most distasteful business." He paused, removed a monogrammed handkerchief from his breast pocket, wiped his forehead, then his moist white hands. In a swift action, he folded it expertly and returned it to his breast pocket, monogram showing. "So, Mr. Hanks, I must have payment or assurance of payment, or I shall deliver Mr. Becker's body to his wife again, and she may do with it as she will."

"Mr. Matthias—"

"Disgusting business!" the tall man went on. "How is one to make a presentable display with that horrible disfiguring gash? Everyone who approaches the casket will look for it."

"Damn it, that's enough!"

Mr. Matthias flinched at the profanity, but he returned to his chair and sat down, obviously disappointed in the judge.

"Now, sir, I will tell you what we are going to do," said the judge, with an anger in his voice Jody did not recognize. "I will sign, at this moment, an instrument guaranteeing payment of the Becker funeral expenses, providing they are reasonable. You, however, will not disclose that arrangement to Mrs. Becker. As far as her knowledge extends, your negotiations concerning funeral expenses are entirely with her. Is that clear?"

"Perfectly clear, Mr. Hanks," said Mr. Matthias, who recovered his composure with remarkable alacrity and deftly produced a long form from his desk. "Sign here."

The judge, his ears red, signed with a flourish.

"Now," said Mr. Matthias, "would you like to send the lady in?" The paper returned quickly to his desk drawer.

The judge motioned to Jody, who hurried outside. Harry and Rose sat in the back seat of the judge's car. In the still–warm evening the car door stood open. Rose had her head lying over on Harry's shoulder, her eyes closed, a big tear still showing in the wrinkle over her cheek. Jody walked up close and said quietly, "Mr. Matthias says you should come in now, Mrs. Becker."

Rose opened her eyes and sat up slowly. Harry stepped out of the open door ahead of her and gave her his hand. Rose hauled herself out and straightened her dress. They all went into the funeral parlor as into some strange temple, unwillingly.

The judge was waiting for Rose, but Mr. Matthias stepped up quickly, took her from Harry's arm, and ushered her to a chair before his desk. Harry and the judge awkwardly sat down on the lavender sofa. Jody retreated to the shadows where he leaned self–consciously against the wall.

"My dear lady, accept my condolences," Mr. Matthias said soothingly as he seated her and patted her shoulder. "Now, there is just a bit of information we will need for the funeral and the obituary. Ah—that is, unless you have already prepared an obituary?"

"No," Rose said.

"Ah, that's all right, my dear," said Mr. Matthias. Another form came promptly from another drawer. "We shall fill in the blank places with the appropriate information, and I shall have it sent to the newspaper in the morning. Now, are there kin who need to be notified?"

"No, nobody, leastwise nobody we know where is."

"Then we can proceed to the funeral, can't we?"

He chatted easily, steering Rose expertly through the routine. Rose responded almost automatically. When shall the funeral be? Tomorrow would be rather impossible. Shall we say the next day, then? Did Mr. Becker have a suit that could be used? No? Then we can provide one, if that would be satisfactory? Yes. No, Mr. Becker was not a member of any church. No, she didn't know any preacher she wanted to do the service, or any singers. Yes, whatever Mr. Matthias arranged would be just fine. Would Mr. Hanks and this other gentleman (what's your name, sir?), Mr. Bewley, be acceptable pallbearers? Whom else would we like? Rose looked around at the judge.

"We'll get the boys at the marshal's place, if you like, Rose," the judge said.

"Not the marshal," Rose said. "Jody, if he'll do it fer me, and we'll ask Art."

Jody nodded, a little uneasy. Rose gave Mr. Matthias all the names as he wrote them down.

"And now," said Mr. Matthias, the preliminaries over, "would you like to choose a casket?"

Rose began to twist the hem of her dress. "Mr. Matthias," she said, then stopped abruptly. "I ain't got much money," she went on at last, "and I won't have it to pay you till I get things settled up."

"How much are you inclined to spend?" asked Mr. Matthias, his voice even.

"Well, I was wondering if I could do something fer about three hunnert dollars."

Mr. Matthias pursed his lips slightly. On Jody's right, Harry stirred.

"Indeed, Mrs. Becker," said the funeral director dryly, "that would be rather inadequate."

"Maybe I could go four," Rose said.

Mr. Matthias sighed, pushed back his chair and got to his feet. "Let's look at some caskets, shall we?" He came around the desk. This time he did not take Rose's arm. "This way, please," he said over his shoulder as he strode off.

Rose got up awkwardly. Harry and the judge scrambled to her side, each taking an arm, and Jody walked behind. They followed Mr. Matthias into the maze of the building, down a dim corridor along the side of the chapel to a room lighted with fluorescent tubes where several caskets stood open. Jody furtively looked into one before he thought, but they were all empty. The sheen from its lining was like dew on the morning meadow.

"This one is real nice," Rose said, laying her hand tentatively on an ornate bronze casket. "How much is this?"

"That one is twelve hundred ninety-five," said Mr. Matthias, all business. "That is the casket only, of course."

Rose removed her hand. "Maybe you better show me which one I could afford."

Mr. Matthias cleared his throat. "These two," he said, laying his hands on two at the far end of the room, "are our least expensive models. The plainer one is three hundred, the other four seventy-five."

Rose drew a deep breath. Resolutely she turned to the plain model. She came up close to it, leaned over it, and looked inside. Then she patted the cushioned place where Bill's head would lie. She was staring into the casket as if trying to envision him lying there.

"It's real nice," she said at last. She glanced aside at the other casket, on which Mr. Matthias' left hand was still at rest. "Except fer the trim and all, they's about alike, ain't they?"

"The trim, as you call it," said Mr. Matthias, "is only part of the difference. This superior model, with its advanced construction and materials, is designed to be more effective in keeping out ground water for an extended time."

"Ground water?" Rose said. A flash of pain went over her face. She looked down into the casket with a slowly dawning comprehension. "Ground water! To keep out the ground water!" Suddenly she began to laugh, a low, horrifying, alto laugh, a dry, croaking sound with a growing anger in it. "What in hell for?" Her shouted words echoed through the big building.

"You bastard," Harry said to Mr. Matthias.

Rose didn't need his help. She walked over to the amazed mortician, took the lid of his superior model, and slammed it shut with a force that surely tested its advanced construction. Over the closed casket, in the empty silence that followed the echoing slam of its elegant lid, Mr. Matthias looked into the burning eyes of Rose Becker, like a bird fascinated by a snake.

"What in hell for?" Rose said again in controlled rage, her voice down in the tenor register. "Do you think the dead give a good damn whether the ground water gets in?" She walked over to another expensive casket and slammed it with even greater force. "Will your damn casket keep a face from rotting away? Will my Bill open his eyes some morning and see this purple satin? Is he gonna lie there in a bought hole and think how proud he is of all the frilly doodads on his purty box?"

Slowly she was going around the room, punctuating her speech by one violent slam after another. At last she came back around to the last casket, the one she could buy for three hundred dollars, where Mr. Matthias stood, stunned, his right hand still resting on its foot.

"I'll take this coffin," she said, in a calmer voice. "And my old Bill will just have to forgive me fer any discomfort he feels. I wisht I could do more fer you, Honey," she said to the open casket, "but I promise I'll pay the difference in grieving. As fer you," she said, shifting her eyes to Mr. Matthias, "I'll pay you what I've got to, but here's one widow that is gonna tell you, you're a vulture." She spat the word at him. "I'm gonna see about getting me some religion, 'cause I don't want to share Hell with you when I die."

Mr. Matthias dabbed his forehead with his handkerchief, his hand trembling. By the time he had returned the handkerchief to his pocket, he was able to smile wanly.

"There remains a piece of business, Mrs. Becker." His voice had lost its edge, but he held his head erect, and the fluorescent light made his hair glisten. "Where should the deceased be buried?"

Rose dropped her eyes. "I don't have a cemetery lot."

Mr. Matthias waited a few moments. Then he went on in a steadier professional tone. "A lot can be purchased, of course. We have a good variety available, in a range from fifty to four hundred dollars."

Rose did not look him in the face. "How much would I owe you fer the services and this casket and a fifty-dollar lot?"

"Hmm. Well, let us say, with the clothing for the deceased, five hundred ten dollars, including taxes, of course."

"Including taxes," Rose said. She studied the floor another moment, and then looked at the judge. "There's no way anybody will give me five hunnert dollars fer that car. My old friend, I hate to ask, you know how much I do, but do you think you could loan me maybe two hunnert against the deed to my old house?"

"Sure, Rose. Whatever you need."

"Then let's call it done," she said to Mr. Matthias. "When should I come back to see my Bill?"

"By tomorrow noon," said Mr. Matthias, all business once more. "By which time I will have all papers prepared for your signature."

Rose had turned and was walking back into the corridor. Harry rushed to walk beside her, the judge and Jody fell in behind, and Mr. Matthias finished his sentence to himself as he snapped off the light.

Chapter Nine

They delivered Rose to Mrs. Gamble with the agreement that the judge would be back in the morning to help her take the Buick to Ashton and sell it. He would bring her home after she had been to see Bill's body.

As they clambered back into the DeSoto, Harry said to the judge, "Now, if you've got a monkey wrench, we can go by and get that money from Bill's car. It'll take me about five minutes."

"Harry," the judge said, "we can't afford to have me, or Jody, mixed up in anything that might look illegal. You or Rose may need to make use of me before this business is over."

"It was my money," said Harry. "I put it there afore I went overseas. I left it fer Bill and Rose fer a wedding present. I wrote him from Germany while he was still in prison and told him it was there, but I got the letter back marked "return to sender" in Bill's handwriting and I never tried again to tell him about it. I've still got that letter. It ain't been opened."

"Where did you get two thousand dollars?"

Harry chuckled. "I refuse to answer that question on account in some folks' mind it might tend to incriminate me. Did I answer that'n right, counselor? Besides, all that was in my other life. I'll tell you that it wasn't stole. Let's just say that Bill and me stumbled on a chance to turn some easy money by buying cheap and selling high, like other business folk. That two thousand is what's left of my half—what I didn't drink up or throw away. I kind of lived like a prodigal son fer a while there after the marriage while I was hurting about it so bad. Bill and Rose been living off his half fer the last four year."

The judge pulled the DeSoto to a stop in the road away from the Becker house. "Okay," he said, getting out. He went to the trunk of his car and fumbled in the dark through a bag of tools and handed Harry the wrench. "Jody and I will wait here. If you hear the car start up and leave, that means somebody was coming, and you should look sharp to take cover. We'll be back by after it's safe."

"I won't be long," Harry said, and then he was gone.

"If we get out of all this without somebody getting hurt or going to jail," the judge said to Jody, "I hope you and I learn to keep out of other people's business hereafter."

"Looks to me like Harry and Rose would of had a hard time without your help."

"You're probably right." The judge sighed. "There doesn't seem to be much way to help people from a safe distance, so what else can you do? You either get in or get out. I'll tell you something, my young accomplice, that you won't learn in Sunday school, or in law school either for that matter, or in mortician's school, or any other school I know about. When you do get in, it's going to cost you something. Most of all, it will likely cost you a clear conscience, if you keep being honest with yourself. That's something I found out on the bench, and I've puzzled over it all my life since. You are seldom able to do right without doing something wrong in the same act."

Tired as he was, something came alert deep in the wells of Jody's mind. He was struggling to grapple with it. "We ought to do right."

"I know," the judge said.

"But what does it mean?"

"I don't think I know. Maybe there are two different kinds of right. There's a kind that goes by rules and keeps the world orderly, and without it life would be a jungle. But when it gets its way altogether, it grinds people up, and it can't tell the difference between a kindly heart and a vicious one. There's another kind of right that sees somebody hurting and demands that you do something, whatever the rules are. So you have to do something, but sure enough, you often wind up doing about as much harm as good. And likely you lose your own integrity as well when you get honest about your motives."

Jody thought about that for a minute. "Ain't there some way to do right both ways at once?"

"Aha!" the judge said in a low, satisfied voice. "I surely hope so. You've got to keep trying to find the way or make a way. However, don't expect it to be easy, and don't expect it to work out all the time."

A soft step came down the driveway form the house. "Here's Harry," Jody said.

"I got it," Harry said, giving the wrench back to the judge. Something oblong and dark was tucked under his arm. The judge put the wrench back in the truck. They slid into the DeSoto and pulled away.

"You want to keep this at yore place?" Harry asked.

"I'd rather not, if you can find some other place to put it."

"Where could it be put where it wouldn't get lost or found or stole?"

Jody said, in a flash of insight, "In the marshal's garage."

They all laughed together. "That's good," Harry said. "If he's gonna keep me penned up, I can watch out fer Rose's money at the same time."

The judge let them out at the marshal's store. It was black inside but Jody showed Harry where to scale the back fence and let him in by the back door he had propped open. The stench of the animals hit them like a blow.

"It's dark as hell in here," Harry said as he stepped inside.

"Don't move around," Jody said. "You'd likely step off into the pit. Let me get a light on. I can find my way in the dark."

"I'll strike a match."

"No, don't do that. There's too much oil and grease in everything," Jody said. "If something should catch, we'd have a bonfire afore we knowed it." He felt his way along the familiar objects until he found the switch by the office door. The garage and pit sprang into light. Harry was blinking his eyes and standing in the corner by the back door, the animals and birds awake and watching them. Harry had a mud-stained metal box under his arm. He came forward and sat down on the steps going down into the pit and looked at the box.

It had been a fancy candy box or cookie tin. It was so dirty and rusted that nothing could be made of the lettering on its outside.

There was a bright yellow stripe around the middle, though. "That's where the strap–iron was that I bolted it on with," Harry said, running his finger around the stripe. "It's rusted plumb through in places. Good thing I wrapped the money careful." He pulled off the lid. The can folded and bent under his fingers but stayed intact. He took out a pouch made from a piece of raincoat and tied up with a thong. Inside that was another pouch of leather, in which was an envelope made of the raincoat and sewed up together. Harry pulled it open carefully. Inside was a packet wrapped in wax paper. When he opened the paper there was a small bundle of bills.

"Well," said Harry, "they're a bit brittle, but they're all right. Rose ain't quite as poor as she thinks."

He put the money back in the leather pouch, put it in the box, and pushed the lid back in place. He looked around the garage for an inconspicuous spot and finally tucked it behind some rusted coffee cans filled with bolts and washers on a shelf near the door, about a foot above eye level.

"Do you think that'll be noticed?" he asked.

"No reason fer it to be. Ain't nobody looked at them cans all summer."

"Okay," said Harry, satisfied. "Let's find a place to settle and get some sleep. I'm plumb wore out, and I know you've had a hard day. Where do we sleep around here?"

"In the office," said Jody, leading the way. He pulled his grimy bedroll out of its place and spread out his pallet. "We can share," he said.

Harry was quiet a moment. "You go right ahead. I think it's gonna be too hard on the concrete fer old bones like mine. You lie down and sleep. I'm gonna sleep sitting in the marshal's chair."

Jody began to protest, but Harry dropped down in the chair and settled motionless, his feet propped on the desk. Jody shrugged, returned to the garage to turn off the light, and groped his familiar path to the pallet. It really was too narrow to sleep two, he thought to himself as he pulled off his shoes and lay down.

But he was restless. For one thing, the marshal's chair creaked from time to time, and so he knew Harry was still awake. But besides that, it was a new and insistent sensation, the sense of Harry being there. Before there had been only Jody and the smells and the random sounds the birds and animals sometimes made. After ten minutes, he said, "You still awake, Mr. Bewley?"

"The name's Harry. Anybody's shared with me like you has calls me Harry. Now Mr. Matthias," he spat the word out, "him and his like calls me Mr. Bewley. Anyone calls you Mr. Carpenter, Jody, you keep a sharp eye on him, 'cause he's gonna do you a mischief pretty soon."

Jody grinned in the dark. "Okay, Harry. Can you tell me when is it right to break the law?"

"When the law is wrong," Harry said, not even hesitating.

That took Jody by surprise. He thought about it for half a minute, and then he said, "How can you tell when it's wrong?"

"Oho! Well, now, you just moved from grade school to collitch with that one. That there's a hard question." He was silent a minute. "'Fraid I'm not a very good teacher in this subject. I've done a lot of things was wrong, and I've done some was agin the law. Sometimes they was the same thing. Sometimes they wasn't. Sometimes I thought they wasn't and they was." There was another pause. "Maybe if we work on it we can figure something out. You tell me. What makes a wrong thing wrong?"

Jody sat up on the pallet. The question stunned him. He was about to say he didn't know, but he hated to concede that. He took a stab. "Because the Bible says so."

"Nope," said Harry. "The Bible says so because it's wrong. It's not wrong because the Bible says so. Try again."

"Well, then, because God says so."

"Better, but not good enough. God's got his reasons too, just like the Bible has. Try again."

"I don't know."

"That's right," Harry said. "You don't know and I don't know. Might as well go on to sleep, huh? I'll tell you what we do know, though. It may not be the whole truth, and it may not be nothing but the truth, but it's the truth. Wrong is wrong because it hurts people."

The room was quiet while Jody's mind chewed on that answer. He found it nourishing, but something was still not right. "But sometimes the right thing hurts people too, and sometimes you can't tell what'll hurt and what won't."

Harry chuckled. "Well, well, you're a real philosopher, Jody lad." The chair creaked loud as he put his feet on the floor. "How'd you learn that so young? Before I knew that I had cut a swath of misery as wide as a barn and made scars that ache to this day." He stood up, groped his way to the window, and looked out on Trasherdell's empty, ragged street. "Yes, the right can hurt too. But see here. There's a kind of hurt that leaves people mean and twisted and flaky, and there's a kind that makes them kindly and clean-living and steady-minded. So you see, we ain't talking about the same thing, are we?"

"Did Bill Becker do wrong to kill hisself?"

There was a long, long silence. Harry's silhouette didn't move at all against the glooming window frame.

"Yes," he said at last, "it was wrong. It must not of seemed so to him at the moment. He meant it as a kindness to Rose and maybe to me and maybe to the whole world. You was wrong, old Bill. God forgive you fer it, as I do."

He turned at last and made his way back to the chair. Over the creaking, he spoke again. "And now, son, you've got to sleep. Leave all this fer a while. Like I said, you need a better teacher than me. Find the best man you know and listen well to what he says and go from there. Ain't likely you'll get to the bottom of it all at once, and fer sure not tonight. Sleep, now. The marshal is gonna be here fore you're rested."

Jody tried. His body was weary, but his mind was disturbed. Who was the best man he knew? Suddenly he heard the dead man's words come back to him from last night, "Maybe the best man I ever knew, Josh Carpenter."

The memory steadied him. He had never really thought of his father as unusually wise or good. Of course he was, but living with it day in, day out, he never thought about it.

I'll ask my dad, he said to himself, and something inside said yes.

Still he was not at peace. Then he remembered he hadn't prayed. He pulled his body again to his knees and numbered to himself those he wished God's care upon. He didn't know whether it would do any good, but he prayed again for Bill Becker. He lay down again and continued to go over their names and faces in his mind, like the beads of a rosary: Bill, Rose, Harry, Doc, the judge. At last he drifted into sleep. In the night sometime he woke briefly, and in the gloom saw Harry asleep on the floor, curled around the base of the stove.

Chapter Ten

He awoke to the smell of coffee. Harry was up and had started the pot. The first color of dawn was showing through the east window. He would be up and ready for work today when the marshal came.

He carried the cleaner clothes he had worn to Ashton into the garage and hung them carefully on a nail in the corner. Then he put on the rumpled and smelly clothes he had worn yesterday. The clean clothes had to be saved for the funeral if he was going to be a pallbearer. As he pulled on his shoes, he had a moment of panic and guilt. Shouldn't he tell Harry about the footprint? Wouldn't it be safer for Harry to know? He added up all the explanations he would have to make, all the secrets he would have to share, and it was too much of a risk. Harry would be angry and hurt and would despise him for being a nasty little sneak, and, thought Jody, he'd be right.

"There's something mighty serious on yore mind," Harry said.

It startled him. As he looked up, he saw that Harry had been studying his face. He felt his color change a little, and he dropped his eyes.

"Hey, little buddy," said Harry with a laugh, "don't take the world so hard. So you gotta go pick up garbage, and I gotta keep the possum company a while longer. They's worse things."

"Yeah," Jody said, with a weak grin. "I need to give the animals some fresh water. It's gonna be a hot morning afore we finish up and get back."

He grabbed his bucket and went to the pump, glad to have a reason to be out of Harry's presence until he could straighten out his thoughts. He made the rounds quickly, speaking to each one of the animals. The barred owl was dead. Jody tried not to think about that for the moment, but continued his rounds. Nellie was nuzzling her last pup. Rupe met him with a stretch and a yawn, waving his thick brush at him.

How thin he's getting, Jody thought sadly. He always made Rupe's station last so he could talk with him a moment. Harry came to the back door and watched him.

"His name's Rupe," Jody said. "Ain't he a fine dog, now? Too bad about that leg."

"All of us got a handicap of some kind," Harry said.

"I got to bury the owl," Jody said. He put up his water bucket, took the shovel from the corner, and took the owl from the cage in the pit. All the other birds and animals watched him somberly. Harry walked with him into the weedy lot and brushed the owl's feathers with his fingers as Jody dug a hole.

"Like I said," Harry mused, "they's worse things."

They went back to the office. Harry poured himself another cup of coffee and offered Jody some. Jody didn't drink coffee, but he nodded just for the sake of camaraderie. They sat quietly, sipping the strong brew, and waited for the marshal. Within a few minutes the truck pulled up. They saw him get out, then stop short as he smelled the coffee. He opened the door slowly and stood gawking at Harry.

"Come in and have a cup," Harry said. "As you can see, the sheriff sent me back. It seems you forgot to sign my papers and he couldn't lock me up without them. You know how these big–town lawmen are. It looks like I'll have to board with yore possum yet a while."

The marshal grunted and poured himself a cup of coffee. He handed Jody a paper sack and said to Harry, "Well, we need to get this investigation completed soon. The city of Trasherdell can't afford to feed prisoners fer very long. Fer now, uh, Jody, you'll be willing to share yore breakfast, like you did yesterday, I'm sure. We'll get you something more to eat after a while."

Jody opened the sack. There were four biscuits, burned on the bottom, and some cold oatmeal in a fruit jar. Jody spread out the sack for a napkin and put the biscuits on it. There was only one spoon for the oatmeal.

"I never could eat oatmeal since my mama made me when I was a kid," Harry said. 'I'll have one o' them homemade biscuits, though. You're a lucky man, Marshal, to have a good woman to cook hot meals fer you." He took a biscuit, dunked it in his coffee, and began to eat.

"Yeah. Well, you better eat fast, unless you want to take it down to the pit with you. Jody and me got to go to work."

"You know, Marshal," Harry said, "you being a public official and all, in a time of emergency, what you need is to be able to stay in the office, near the phone. Don't see why you couldn't cuff me to the steering column, like you did yesterday, and let me drive Jody around."

The marshal paused in midsip. He looked at Harry and then at Jody, but neither one smiled or said anything. At last he put down his cup and walked over behind the desk. He took out the handcuffs and looked at them.

"Supposing you was to just keep driving," he said.

Harry laughed. "Where to? How much gas you got in the tank? What would I do when I ran out?"

The marshal relaxed. "I guess I could do that. I sure enough do need to be near the phone."

Jody was spooning down the cold oatmeal. He decided the oatmeal was all he would have for breakfast. In the first place, by evening it would be hard and crusty and taste even worse than it did now. Besides, it wouldn't keep very well in the heat. If it sat all day, it might make him sick. Most of all, he knew Harry didn't like oatmeal, and it might turn out there wouldn't be any more food. He'd save the biscuits.

When he had finished it, he took a long drink from the bucket and felt full. One thing about cold oatmeal: he wouldn't be hungry for a while.

The marshal put one cuff on Harry's wrist and left the other cuff open.

"Air you telling me to go shackle myself?" Harry said with a grin.

The marshal guffawed. "Go on," he said, "and Jody, don't you let him run away."

They made the run in good time. Jody almost enjoyed himself. Harry clowned and cracked jokes about Jody sorting the garbage. From the truck bed behind, Jody joked back and shouted directions. By the time they got back, Jody was singing to himself the way he used to when he worked in the fields.

In Earthen Vessels

They walked back into the office together. Harry had not bothered to fasten the handcuff to the steering column, so he came in with it dangling open, just as he had left. Johnny, Doc, and the marshal were gathered around the stove. The marshal rose as they came in.

"Here's the chain gang coming back," he said, ostentatiously taking Harry's cuff and snapping it around the arm of the judge's swivel chair. "We'll give him the place of honor in the judge's absence."

They all laughed a little about that. Jody left them to take the food drum around to the back. It had been a good day, but much of the food was spoiled because it hadn't been collected yesterday. Jody sorted again carefully, fed the animals, gave them all clean water, then buried the refuse. He came into the office through the back door, picked up his broom, and began sweeping the back corners.

"Yeah, we're all pallbearers," Harry said, "except the marshal here. Reckon his official duties make it impossible."

"That's not it," Johnny said. "She's pissed off at the marshal fer asking her who her lover was."

Doc laughed. "That may be. Marshal, have you done what she told you to do yesterday?"

"What was that?" Johnny asked.

"Kiss her ass and go to hell," Doc said.

Johnny burst into a loud whoop. "Hey, Marshal, you didn't tell me that part."

"Reckon it slipped my mind," the marshal said. He reached over and spat into the zinc bucket to cover his embarrassment.

"You're barking up the wrong tree there, Marshal," Harry said. "Rose wouldn't trifle on old Bill."

"Well, somebody's been tramping around that house," said the marshal. "What else could it of been?"

"Likely just somebody drifting through looking for something to steal," Doc said.

"They sure looked in the wrong town," Johnny said. "Ain't nothing in Trasherdell worth stealing, and fer sure nothing in the Becker house. Maybe if they'd picked the judge's house, they might of found something."

'It's mighty peculiar," said the marshal, "fer that to happen just when Bill Becker gets killed. It all fits in, somehow."

A car pulled up and stopped. It was a small, sleek red convertible, different from anything Jody had ever seen. A tall man in his early thirties got out and looked around him uncertainly, then stepped slowly into the doorway. He was bronzed and athletic, with white shoes and neat sky blue trousers. He had a gold wrist watch, and his wavy blond hair glistened in the sun. Everyone turned and stared at him.

"I was told at the cafe that this is the Trasherdell Kennels," he said in a rich baritone. He looked quickly around the room, his eyes sweeping the group of men and the furnishings. "Perhaps I'm in the wrong place."

Nobody said a word. He waited a moment, then went on.

"My name is Jason Justice. I've been away, and I boarded my dog at the kennels while I was gone."

The marshal stood up. "Yes sir, Mr. Justice," he said, "this is the place. We didn't expect you back so soon."

"Yes, I'm early," the young man said, stepping on inside. "I got bored with the Mediterranean. I'm going to pick up Rupert and go to the seashore for the rest of the summer. If you'll bring me my dog, please, and calculate my charges."

The marshal was nervous, but he bluffed it through. "Mr. Carpenter, will you go get Rupert, that's the fine chow-chow in run number three, for this gentleman. Mr. Justice, will you be seated a minute?"

Mr. Justice looked at the grimy chair where the marshal had been sitting. "No, thank you," he said, "I'll just stand."

Jody hurried from the room. From a nail on the wall, he took the studded collar and leash Rupe had worn when the marshal brought him in. He hurried to the pen, put the collar on while Rupe licked his face, and brought him out. On an inspiration, he grabbed the comb and brush and went quickly over Rupe's coat, trying to brush out as much of the dirt and tangles as he could. "I'm gonna miss you," he told the dog. Quickly he tossed the comb and brush aside and led Rupe back to the office.

"Here he comes," the marshal said as the dog was brought in.

Mr. Justice looked at his dog in disbelief. Rupe gave him a friendly bark and waved his tail, but the owner did not acknowledge it. Slowly, slowly, he walked around Rupe, looking him over. A red flush was showing through his tan, and his fist was clenched.

"What have you done to my dog?" he said. The sentence began intensely and ended in a sharp crescendo.

"Why, what's the matter, Mr. Justice?" the Marshal said.

"The matter! Look at him!" For the first time he reached a hand toward the dog, gave him a quick perfunctory pat, but ran his fingers through the ruff around his neck, along his ribs. Then he stood up, wiped his hand on a handkerchief he took from his hip pocket, and turned glaring eyes on the marshal.

"He's dirty," he said. "He's so thin I can feel his ribs. What do you feed him, straw? He's losing patches of his fur. He must have a mange!"

"Why, Mr. Justice, you're surely mistaken," said the marshal, his voice a little desperate. "Why he's fit as a fiddle, ain't you, Rupert? It's just the heat, and chows, you know, they're so heavy coated they have to shed, and you don't want to overfeed them in weather like this. Oh, I see!" He leaned over the dog. "He ain't been brushed down today, maybe not fer two days! Mr. Carpenter, I've warned you I won't tolerate you not keeping the dogs groomed. I'm surely going to have to let you go fer this!" He turned on Jody with a menace in his eyes.

Mr. Justice jerked his head backward as though he had been slapped. "What kind of fool do you think I am, you stupid ass? I've shown prize dogs in three states. Don't try to flimflam me. A dog doesn't get in that shape without extended neglect. What kind of place is this?"

Before the marshal could stop him, he had gone through the door into the garage. He stopped dead still in the doorway, his face registering his disbelief and disgust. He turned his eyes upon Jody in one glance of horror and accusation. Then he turned back on the marshal, his eyes flashing.

"Now, Mr. Justice, we also deal in unusual animals, and we got all kinds here, but we been taking real good care of Rupert." The marshal's voice was getting insistent. "Why old Rupert gets the best food we got, and we care fer him like a baby, don't we, Rupe?" He came near the dog, and in spite of a throaty growl reached a hand to pat him on the head.

Rupe gave a sharp, vicious snarl and ripped the marshal's hand from the heel to the base of his little finger.

There was a shocked silence. Rupe's ruff stood up around his neck, and he watched the marshal steadily. Jody still held his leash.

"Gawd almighty," said the marshal, as blood began to drip profusely from the wound.

Doc jumped to his feet. "I'll get my kit," he said, and trotted from the room.

Now the marshal was angry. He held his left wrist to dull the pain and wheeled on Mr. Justice. "You pay me the sixty dollars you owe me fer boarding this animal," he said, "and you take that chow son of a bitch and put him in yore pretty little kiddy car and you get out of my town and don't bring him back, and maybe I won't sue you fer all you got."

"Don't threaten me," said Mr. Justice, "and don't talk nonsense. I'm not going to pay you for ruining my dog. I'm not going to put that mangy, dirty dog in my car. I'm not going to take him back at all. He's turned vicious, little wonder, and he'll have to be destroyed. You're going to pay for it, stupid. I'm going to put you out of business. You'll be hearing from me."

He brushed past Doc, just back with his kit, and strode out the door. The little red convertible roared into life and slung gravel behind it as he sped away.

"Nasty tear," Doc said, rinsing it with alcohol. "We're going to have to take stitches, Marshal. Maybe you should go into Ashton where you can get a shot for anesthetic."

"Shit," the marshal said, "it already hurts like the devil. A few stitches ain't gonna make any difference. Sew it up."

Doc got his curved needle and some catgut from the kit, washed everything in alcohol, and stitched his hand.

"I'm gonna kill me a dog," the marshal said while Doc sewed, his eyes fixed on Rupe.

Rupe stared right back at him, a growl rumbling in his throat.

"Don't growl at me, damn you!" he said.

Rupe growled again, louder, and showed his teeth.

"Take him out of here, Jody," Harry said. "Put him back in his pen."

Jody's eyes appealed to Harry. Harry shook his head, slightly. Jody said, "Come on, Rupe." The dog turned and followed him from the room, watching the marshal all the way. Jody took him back to his pen and slipped the collar from his neck. He had a tremendous urge to put him through the gate and let him go, but he shut the pen and returned the collar and leash to its place on the wall.

As he came back, Doc was still at work. The marshal was sweating heavily, but he didn't cry out as the needle made its punctures.

"Look at it this way," Harry said. "It's still Justice's dog. If you kill him, you'll only make Justice mad, and he's got a real strong case agin you. Otherwise, likely you won't hear from him again. Man like that, he don't need money, and he don't care about the dog, and he just won't want to bother. He'll write a letter or two, and then let it drop. If he tries to get you in trouble, he's got to stay around and make himself a nuisance. He'd rather be at the beach."

"Now let me tell you something, Harry," the Marshal said. "That shit–kicking dog like to took my hand off. I'm gonna take my pistol and put it up his asshole—"

"And what'll that prove?" Harry said. "I give you credit for being smarter than that. Why, be practical, man. You got yourself a registered, pedigreed sire. Why, he's a gold mine. You don't have to love him, fer Christ's sake. Jody can handle him. All you need to do is advertise his services and hire you a banker."

The marshal was still flushed in the face, but he was studying something. "What kind of fee do you think I could charge?"

"Why, if you feed him good and sleek him up, I'd say fifty, sixty dollars. Wouldn't you say so, Johnny?" His eyes urged Johnny to go along.

"Sure, maybe more, a hunnert, maybe, if you found the right people."

"I'd have to get the papers," the marshal said.

"Well, smart man like you, you could do that. Get back in touch with Justice. Tell him you need to own the dog outright afore you can have it destroyed. It'll work out."

Doc finished the last stitch. "I'll give you some pills to take the edge off the pain, but along about tomorrow evening you're gonna be pretty uncomfortable."

"Yeah. Well, it won't be the first time. How much do I owe you?"

"Tell you what," Doc said, "I want to get a litter of pups for my grandniece. You let me bring the bitch around in a month or two and put your chow to stud, and we'll call it even, okay?"

"Yeah, okay," the marshal said. He got up and flexed his hand a little.

"We'll put a bandage around that," Doc said, "and you better put a glove over it to keep it clean." He wound gauze deftly around the hand.

"I'll go by home and get a cotton glove. Then I guess I better get back to the Becker house and get my investigation finished." He turned, went out the door, climbed into his truck, and drove away.

"Thanks, Johnny," Harry said. "Thanks to you too, Doc."

Johnny shook his head. "I'd of never believed it. You're a con man, Harry. You ought to be in the state legislature."

"Oh no," Harry said. "You're not giving the marshal enough credit."

"Maybe so, but sounded to me like he wanted to kill that dog."

"Sure he did, fer a minute. Mostly he was just feeling put down. He needed a way to save face."

"Harry," Doc said, "do you really think he can make any money from that dog?"

"I dunno, Doc, but I'll tell you one thing. He's already paid his doctor bill."

They all had a good laugh.

"Yeah," Doc said. "Now I've got to find a bitch to give my grandniece."

Chapter Eleven

It was almost dawn. In the gloom, Jody saw Harry curled around the stove, as he had been the night before, except this time he was handcuffed to one of the stove legs. Jody lay unmoving on his pallet and thought of the coming day. It was the day they would bury Bill Becker.

The judge had come by in the evening and had a long talk with Harry and Jody. Rose had sold the car for three hundred dollars and borrowed enough from the judge to pay Mr. Matthias. The judge declined a mortgage on the ramshackle Becker house. Rose had spent an hour alone with Bill Becker's corpse where it lay in its casket in the alcove of the funeral home. The judge had gone to the florists meanwhile and ordered a wreath of carnations.

Jody lay imagining Bill in his casket with his head resting where Rose had patted the lining. He wondered how Mr. Matthias, or whoever did it, had sewed up the gash in the throat, like Doc sewing up the marshal's hand (except it didn't hurt Bill). He tried to imagine what it would look like, but the picture of the great gaping wound he had seen kept coming to his mind, and he fled from it. Then he remembered how the right arm was flung out from the bed, already stiff when they carried him out to the hearse, and wondered how they got that arm back where it was supposed to be in the casket. Did they have to break it to make it fold in across his chest the way dead people were supposed to lie?

He thought about Bill having dirt thrown over him, having the sound of clods on his coffin and not hearing them. What is it like to lie in a box with dirt over you forever or anyway until the last judgment, whenever that was? When God said Rise, Arise would Bill Becker try to push open his coffin with his broken arm? Or would he simply rise up through metal and wood and earth to stand before God with his throat sewed together, trying to sing "Worthy is the Lamb" like it said in Revelation?

A shaft of red sunlight fell across the room. It was time to rise. Jody sat up and pulled on his shoes. Harry was awake at once. His body didn't move but his eyes flew open, and he stared at Jody.

"Thought I ought to get up and put out water fer the animals," Jody said. "If we get to the funeral by ten, I got to hurry around."

Harry sat up. With his right hand he lifted the stove leg two inches and then pulled his left hand away, dragging the handcuffs free. He stood up and stretched himself, the handcuffs dangling from his left wrist. Jody took his bucket, Harry took the coffee pot, and they went to the pump. Harry pumped the pot nearly full of water and went back to make coffee while Jody filled his bucket. Harry stopped by Rupe's cage for a moment and grinned at him.

"Good morning, chow dog," he said. "You damn near got yourself in a passel of trouble yesterday."

Rupe lay with his stump across his good leg and looked at Harry. After a moment, he waved the brush of his tail at him slowly two times. Harry grinned again.

"You don't seem to take the marshal serious enough. Mustn't bite the hand that feeds you." Rupe yawned and rose to stretch. Harry chuckled and went back inside.

Jody quickly gave all the animals water, his mind busy with the funeral. When he went back to the office, Harry sat on Johnny's crate, cradling a cup of coffee in his hands, looking somber. Jody's cup sat steaming on the marshal's desk. He picked it up and sat down self–consciously.

"The marshal ought to be here by now," he said. "Wish he'd hurry up."

"Yeah," Harry said. "I hope he don't make me any problem about going to the funeral. I was gonna talk to him yesterday about it, only he left kind of sudden, and it didn't seem to be a good time to ask. I'll tell you one thing, I'm going whether he wants me to or not."

They sipped their coffee together as the minutes ticked by. Jody got more and more nervous. Finally he stood up.

"I got to do my work. Them animals has to eat. I can't go off and leave them with nothing to eat."

Harry nodded. "Tell you what. Load them drums into my truck. I'll write the marshal a note and tell him where we're gone." He started rummaging in the marshal's desk for a scrap of paper.

Jody ran to the back lot and dragged the drums, two at a time, around to where Harry's truck was. By the time he had them loaded, Harry came through the door, the handcuffs dangling. Jody clambered into the back while Harry slid under the wheel.

"Take it easy," Jody said. "Them drums ain't tied down. We got to hurry, though."

They worked quickly. By the time they came back, the Marshal was there. He was sitting behind the desk, sipping his coffee, his left hand tied up in a cotton rag. His long face was drawn and ugly, and he moved his hand with studied care. Jody gave him one glance and turned immediately to his work. He didn't stop to bury the refuse, he could do that later, but quickly parceled out breakfast to the animals and then washed himself at the pump. It occurred to him that he hadn't eaten anything.

He went into the office through the garage, took his clean clothes from the nail, and stepped back into the garage to change. He could hear Harry through the door, pleading his case.

"I got to go. Rose has asked me to be a pallbearer, and I'm needed to make up the number. Hell, you can come along and watch me all the time, can't you? You know good and well I ain't going anywheres. If I was gonna run away, I'd been gone long ago. C'mon, Marshal, be sensible!"

The marshal didn't say anything. Jody came into the office and sat down in the corner. The marshal didn't say anything to Jody either. He looked at him across his cigarette, held between swollen fingers of his left hand. With his other hand, he set down the cup, poured himself more coffee, and picked it up again.

Outside the judge's DeSoto pulled up, Rose and Mrs. Gamble in the back seat. Behind his car, Doc's Chevy pulled in with Johnny and Art on the seat beside Doc. The judge got out and came inside.

"Time to go," he said. He had on a tie and coat and his shoes were shined. He took off his Panama hat and mopped his balding head with a handkerchief. It was already hot.

Harry didn't move, and Jody sat still, waiting for his cue. The judge stopped mopping his head for a moment, then put his handkerchief away and stood waiting too.

The marshal laid his cigarette down carefully on the handle of his cup. Slowly he got up and came around the desk. With his good hand he took a key and opened the handcuff, not the one fastened around Harry's wrist, but the one dangling from the short chain. With a jerk of his head, he motioned for Jody. Jody stood up uncertainly and came toward him. With one motion, the Marshal reached out the open cuff and snapped it on Jody's left wrist. That done, he returned to his seat, put the cigarette back carefully between his fingers, and picked up his cup.

They all stared at him a moment. Then the judge shrugged and turned toward the door. "Come on," he said.

Harry followed him, trailing Jody behind. Jody had to walk closely and thoughtfully behind Harry not to stumble. By taking care, they could keep the cuffs from showing much. They slid carefully into the front seat of the DeSoto beside the judge. They had to turn around and back into the seat, Jody sliding in first, keeping his left arm stretched across his body to hold his left wrist close to Harry. Rose and Mrs. Gamble seemed not to notice.

Rose had another dress on, one Jody had seen in her closet. Mrs. Gamble had tried to fix Rose's hair, but instead of curling like it ought to it had just frizzled into little clumps. She was crying, a voiceless, labored cry, the cry of someone who has cried for hours unable to stop, her body heaving involuntarily. Mrs. Gamble patted Rose's big arm with her thin leathery fingers, her eyes watery behind her horn–rimmed glasses, her bony knees making two knobs under her flour–sack print dress.

Nobody tried to talk to Rose, she was so completely in the grip of her heavy dry sobbing, but Mrs. Gamble kept saying "now, now" in a soft voice. Those words and the sobs and the throb of the motor made a little trio of sad sounds, a counterpoint of raw grief. In spite of himself, Jody stared over his shoulder at Rose, her eyes closed, her shoulders heaving in a cruel rhythmic pattern. It reminded him of something, the way her body heaved and fell in its unconscious cadence. Only when she began rocking to and fro did he remember with a sudden horror what it was.

Finally, about halfway to Ashton, Rose's long sobs evened out into a deep and regular breathing, like a child going to sleep. She wiped her face on a big handkerchief and stuffed it back in the bosom of her dress.

"Bill looked real nice," she said in a husky voice. "He looked as peaceful, like he'd just gone to sleep. I sat there and combed his hair. Mr. Matthias has done a good job on him, anyway. I got to give him that."

"Now, now," Mrs. Gamble said. She was still patting Rose's arm.

"I just hope it's a nice funeral. Bill would of liked his coffin—casket, I mean."

"Someday," Harry said, "we'll get Bill a stone."

"That'd be real nice," Rose said.

The DeSoto pulled up in front of Matthias' Funeral Parlor. Doc's troupe pulled up right behind them. Everybody got out and trooped inside, Jody standing close behind Harry so the handcuffs wouldn't show very much.

Mr. Matthias, in a black suit, came from behind his desk. He gave a quick glance of distaste at Harry and Jody, who didn't have suits on, but turned immediately to Rose and Mrs. Gamble, pushing them gently down the aisle toward the very front where the top half of the casket stood open. The judge's wreath of carnations rested on the lid where it closed over Bill's paunch. There were no other flowers. There was an electronic organ playing somewhere. Mr. Matthias seated the two women and came back where the pallbearers stood in a bunch. He gathered them all around him and began speaking softly.

"Now, men, let me instruct you in your duties—" He stopped abruptly and stared at the handcuffs on Harry and Jody. "Why—what is this?"

The judge cleared his throat. "Mr. Bewley is in custody, but has been allowed to attend the services as a pallbearer."

Mr. Matthias gave Harry one incredulous look, then Jody, then the judge.

"This is preposterous!" he said, raising his voice.

"Sh," the judge said.

"It'll be okay," Harry said in a soft voice. "I got it all figgered out. Jody and me needs to be on the same side of the coffin. We need to be on the left side so's we can carry it with our right hands. Someone, you, Doc, can walk in front, and we'll hold our left hands close together, and won't nobody notice."

Mr. Matthias threw his hands up in a gesture of helplessness and turned away from them. In a moment, though, he readjusted his tie and cuffs and turned back to face them.

"All right. All right! Now when everyone has passed by to view the body, I'll signal you to come up and take the casket to the hearse. There will then be a limousine to take you to the grave site. When you get there, you will take the casket—"

"So Jody and me needs to sit right beside Doc," Harry said. "Here, Doc, you come and stand in front, so's we can go down in the right order. Now, where do you want us to sit? Right behind Rose— uh, Mrs. Becker?"

"Yes, yes. Go sit!" said Mr. Matthias, again too loud. He clenched his fist and walked away, leaving them to file down and find their own places.

They slid into the pew behind Rose and Mrs. Gamble. There were no other people in the chapel. Jody looked steadfastly at Bill Becker's profile in the satin–lined coffin. Bill was all decked out in a suit, the white collar of his shirt pulled up close around the chin. Maybe that was what made his face look strange. It was Bill Becker, all right, but it was someone else too, someone Jody had never seen. He didn't look asleep, he looked grim, with his mouth drawn shut in a line and his skin a funny dead color. Yet he looked dignified, not because of the clothes but in spite of them, in spite of the foolish fuss that was being made, which he couldn't change or evade but in which he stubbornly refused to join. There was a message in his face, if Jody could only figure out what it was.

The music annoyed Jody. The organ and the organist were hidden from them behind a wall. It wasn't a pretty sound, like the treadle organ in the church, but a harsh, metallic quavering, too insistent, too arrogant, as though its own voice was the important thing instead of the song it sung. Jody could make out "I'll Fly Away" and "Beautiful Isle of Somewhere," but the melodies were all misshapen with frilly runs and drawn–out rhythms. He had an urge to go tell whoever was playing not to do that, but he knew that like Bill Becker he must simply endure it all.

He looked around the chapel and saw the sheriff had come in. Art's family was there with a neighbor, and three or four others. That was all. From behind the wall, somebody started singing in a loud, straight soprano, while the organ made quavery noises. It was "When the Roll Is Called up Yonder" but Jody had never heard it sung like that. When she came to the chorus the singer tried to fit in all the parts, soprano and alto and tenor, so it went "when the roll, when the roll, is called" and so on. Afterward there was a short pause while the organ slid down into another key, and she started in on "Whispering Hope." She couldn't quite reach the high notes and couldn't get the low notes either.

After "Whispering Hope" there was a quiet, except for a little snuffling from Rose and Mrs. Gamble's "now, now" in low tones. Then from behind the wall walked a tall, thin man with haunted eyes, his black hair with streaks of gray, a worn black Bible open in his right hand. He stood on the dais and leaned over the podium, looking right down on Bill Becker in his casket. For fully half a minute he said nothing, just stared at the dead man. An eerie quiet settled through the chapel. Then he began to speak.

"In the fourteenth chapter of the Revelation that came to John, we have these holy words in the thirteenth verse: 'Blessed are the dead which die in the Lord from henceforth: Yea, saith the Spirit, that they may rest from their labours; and their works do follow them.'"

He closed the Bible and laid it down on the podium. His glance swept his small audience appraisingly. Slowly, as his eyes came back to Rose, he began shaking his head gently, then began speaking, softly at first, but gathering force as his message carried him away.

"In this hour of loss, our hearts yearn to comfort those who grieve, and we search for some word of encouragement and hope. So has it always been in the grim contest between love and death. But the spirit of the Lord requires a word of truth in this hour. This most serious of all human experiences must not be falsely encountered. We must not lie about what we do here today, for this is a moment of eternal significance.

"So did the beloved apostle write of that great judgment, where we must all stand before the Lord and render our account. The scripture tells us that it is appointed to man once to die, and after that the judgment. We know that one day this body must fail us and we shall be put in the earth and become once again the earth from which we were made. Nobody can escape it or delay it. Just as Bill Becker is this day, so shall we all be in our due time.

"Then, my friends, we will each stand before that great judge and be tried for the life we have lived, and what a trial it will be! There will be no hiding of the evidence from him. There will be no perversion or twisting of the law after the manner of men. No silver-tongued attorney will help us call good evil and evil good. There will be no plea bargaining; there will be no conniving to get a jury that will be prejudiced in our favor; no quibbling over technicalities, no continuations, no change of venue. Truth itself will measure us and sound the depth of our iniquities, and it will be a terrible day."

Jody felt the sweat pop out on his forehead. All his secret sins rose up in his imagination, like witnesses at the judgment. He looked at the dead man, and the grim face seemed to say that he knew all that, and more. Jody would not have been amazed if Bill Becker had sat up at that moment and announced to all that Jody had wickedly looked on his shame.

"Yes!" the voice shouted. "A terrible day! None can endure that day, but those who have been made righteous by the blood of the Lamb. To these the Lord will show mercy; these are they who die in the Lord, as John records, and they shall be blessed, for so shall they ever be with the Lord. But those who must abide his judgment will be cast into everlasting fire.

"And so it is that we have gathered today to note the time when one of us must go to confront his Maker. We must ask ourselves honestly, how is it with him in the presence of the incorruptible judge?"

"Oh my God," Rose said miserably and began to sob softly.

"Oh my poor brother Becker, what defense can you plead before God? What labors do you rest from now, and what works follow you? Your life was spent in lawlessness and marred by violence, and your last act on earth was to fling away like rubbish the precious gift of life, given by God as a means to the salvation of your soul. You threw it away like garbage, and of the temple that was your body you have made a ruin. How stern a judgment you are facing, my poor rebellious brother, and how sad your sentence must be."

Harry stirred uneasily beside Jody, and the shackled hand clenched itself white.

"Now, my friends, we must commit Bill Becker to the earth, and to such judgment as God may be inclined to show, and turn our thoughts again to the living. Whatever Bill Becker was, he is now forever. But oh, my friend, while life is yet yours, that need not be the case with you. I beseech you, dear friend, to reach out to God and lay claim on his promise of mercy, to repent your wickedness, and to bring forth works worthy of repentance! Lest you come at last to the same terrible justice that our poor ruined brother must face."

There arose a wail from Rose Becker that made the hair on Jody's neck stand up, a long anguished cry that reverberated from the walls of the chapel like echoes in a desert canyon, and then another, and another. For all his zeal, the preacher was abashed. He sputtered a few more words, but he was no match for the primordial statement of loss and grief in that animal cry.

He retreated behind the wall, the organ began playing loudly, and Mr. Matthias hurried down to stand by the casket as he urgently motioned the few mourners to rise and troop by. At last the sheriff came up, and the few others after him, and then the pallbearers. Hardly anyone could pay much attention to Bill, for through the whole procedure Rose's insistent wail went on, oblivious, irrepressible, uncomforted.

Hastily a very nervous Mr. Matthias got the pallbearers lined up by the casket, and took Rose and Mrs. Gamble down the aisle ahead of them. Bill was shuffled into the large black Cadillac hearse, Mr. Matthias tucked the two women in the family car with Rose still bawling at the top of her lungs, and the pallbearers were hurried into a limousine. As the small procession pulled out, Jody saw in the car ahead of them Mrs. Gamble's thin arm reach around Rose's huge shoulders.

"I didn't like that funeral much," Harry said.

"Well, I ain't never seen one like it," Johnny Burton said. "That durn preacher, I thought he was getting set to make an altar call. Damned if I don't think he would of done it if Rose hadn't let out such a holler."

"Not that maybe it wasn't all true," Harry said, "but that just wasn't what Rose needed to hear right now."

"I heard him do that once before, at Jenny Abel's funeral," Doc said. "He's always trying to chalk up converts."

"It's my fault," the judge said. "I shouldn't have left it up to Matthias to pick a preacher."

"Minds me of a story," said Johnny. "Did you ever hear the one about the preacher that had to preach this whore's funeral? Seems as how she died during her business hours—"

"Let it be, John," the judge said. "Nobody's in a mood to hear a story now."

They pulled up the long hill to the cemetery and through the rock wall that surrounded it. They passed the huge headstones where the wealthy of other days were buried, passed well–tended plots with the special markers for the veterans of the Civil War, twisted through the graveled lanes until Jody thought they were going to drive right on through. At last there were no more grave plots, no splotches of flowers or greenery. On the far side of the cemetery, in what looked like a meadow, fifty yards from the nearest grave, they came at last to a pile of red clay beside an open hole.

"What's going on?" Harry said. "Why are they burying Bill way out here?"

It was obviously the place. The hearse had stopped; Mr. Matthias was hurrying to the door to open it for the pallbearers. There was no time, no way, to question their roles. They lined up dutifully, picked up the casket, and carried it to the grave. There they set it down on a contraption the likes of which Jody had never seen, but he quickly understood its function. It was going to let Bill down easy into the hole on gentle canvas straps when someone tripped its lever.

Mr. Matthias was gently hurrying Rose and Mrs. Gamble to the folding chairs that sat on a green carpet at the edge of the casket. Rose was preoccupied with her handkerchief and her misery, letting herself be ushered along like a cow driven into a feed lot. Once she had sat down, she began looking about her in bewilderment, as though she weren't sure where she was.

The preacher appeared at the other side of the casket and opened his Bible. In a quiet but intense voice he began to read. He read from Ecclesiastes about all being vanity. Then he read from Romans about the wages of sin being death, and from James about lust bringing forth sin and sin bringing forth death. He read on and on, watching Rose over the edge of his Bible. Rose wasn't listening any more. She was looking around at the small crowd, the hearse, and back to the casket. Then she looked at the ring of blue–stem grass around the trampled and clay–stained place where the grave had been dug.

"What are we doing out here in the pasture?" she said out loud, right through the sound of the preacher's voice. "Why ain't we in the graveyard?"

The preacher kept reading, but faster.

"Get it over with, damn you," Harry's voice said clearly.

The preacher closed his Bible, stepped hurriedly around the casket, and took Rose's hand a second, letting it go quickly to pick up Mrs. Gamble's. After another quick squeeze, he was gone to the hearse like a man in flight. Mr. Matthias came next. When Rose saw Matthias, she grabbed him and gave him a shake.

"Lissen. Hey, lissen. What are you burying Bill out here fer? I paid fer a lot in the cemetery."

Mr. Matthias forced a weak smile and tried to free his lapels from Rose's grip. "My dear Mrs. Becker, this is the cemetery. Do you see that fence over there? That's the property line. Your lot is identified clearly in the agreement we signed."

"But lissen!" Rose's voice was getting desperate. "Not out here like he wasn't good enough to be with other people. Why'd you have to put him way out here by hisself with the prairie dogs and snakes? He was a human being, fer Christ's sake!"

Mr. Matthias wrestled free as Rose collapsed in her chair. She threw up her hands and began the wail again. Mr. Matthias quickly put a few steps between them and straightened his crumpled coat as best he could.

"Mrs. Becker," he said, a bit breathlessly, "Mrs. Becker, my deepest sympathies, and my condolences." He backed away a few steps, then turned quickly and strode to the hearse. He started the motor and swung it in a great circle, bouncing through the tall grass, the preacher beside him, and then he was gone.

Mrs. Gamble and the judge were trying to console Rose. Harry looked steadily at Jody a moment, then gently pulled him aside, away from the little group of confused mourners.

"Little buddy," he said softly, "I'm gonna tell you something none of these people knows. Matthias don't know it neither, nor that vicious son of a bitch that acts like a preacher of the gospel. It's a secret, you see, between me and you. It's got to be kept a secret, except fer one or maybe two others we'll need to tell."

His face was grim, but lit with excitement.

"What is it?" Jody said, in a whisper.

Harry lifted a finger of his free hand, pointing straight up to the sky. He looked around him and looked again at Rose's head, bowed over on her knees, one hand out on the cheap casket with its single wreath of carnations.

"Old Bill," Harry said, shaking his finger, "Old Bill is gonna rise."

Chapter Twelve

They let Rose cry it out for a while as the two men in overalls with shovels respectfully kept their distance behind the mound of red dirt. Then the judge helped her back into the car, and they all left Bill Becker to his divine appointment and went back to the funeral home. There, Harry caught Mrs. Gamble long enough to exchange a quiet word, and when they all got in the cars to go back to Trasherdell Mrs. Gamble was sitting up front with the judge, with Harry and Jody in the back seat with Rose. Jody sat with his left arm pulled across his lap near Harry's left arm, linked to one another as they had been all day. Harry's right arm was around Rose's shoulders, and he was patting and comforting her just as Mrs. Gamble had done.

Once they pulled out on the highway, Jody dropped into a half-doze. He was very tired, and so hungry he felt a little sick. He paid no attention to what Harry was saying to Rose. He probably couldn't have heard him anyway, because Harry talked very low directly into Rose's ear. Rose had stopped crying and was listening to Harry very intently. Now and then she would nod in response. Once Jody saw her hand reach over and squeeze Harry on the shoulder where her head lay.

He thought about Harry's strange prophetic words. What could he mean about Bill going to rise? He had never thought of Harry as a religious man, but the speech had sounded almost mystical. Was Harry talking about the Last Judgment? Was it true about Bill? It was hard to think of God being resentful at Bill for his suicide. It seemed to make God the same kind of person as Mr. Matthias. The preacher had told it straight out of scripture and that was pretty convincing, but surely God could be talked to. The impulse welled up in him and he prayed in his mind. He argued respectfully with the

Lord that maybe Bill meant to do the right thing. Anyway, how can any of us do right all the time? God would have to be forgiving, or nobody could be acceptable. So please, Sir, you've got to forgive Bill Becker if you can. If you can't, I'll try to understand and try to forgive you fer it, but I sure hope you can. Then he thought how silly that was for Jody Carpenter to forgive God, and he grinned to himself. He could almost hear God laughing at his mistake.

The judge let them both out at the animal store and took Rose and Mrs. Gamble home. The marshal was standing in the door watching them slide out together, Harry giving Rose a farewell pat. Jody shot a quick glance at the marshal. It was going to be hard to talk to him today. He held his bandaged hand unnaturally up against his shoulder, keeping it held higher than his arm to relieve the throbbing, and his face was lined and white.

"Well, Marshal," Harry said amiably, "you can see yore deputy brung me back safe. I appreciate yore trusting me enough to let me go, but Bill's casket would of been a bit easier to handle without these shackles."

"Don't get smart," the marshal said. His voice had an edge.

"Okay, okay," Harry said, waving his hands in a conciliatory gesture. The motion tugged Jody's arm and made it wave back and forth too. "Now, hey, don't you think you could break us loose fer a while? No need fer Jody to have to be a prisoner too."

"I'm gonna do just that. Jody's got a lot of work around here he needs to be doing instead of running all over the county like that was what he was paid fer." He took his key and unlocked Jody's cuff. "As fer you, I'm gonna put you back in the pit."

Harry's face fell. "No offense, Marshal, but can't you find me another jail? Not that I got anything against possums, but, lordee, it stinks down there."

"Come on," the marshal said and turned toward the garage. Harry followed him like a dog on a leash.

"Damn it all, Marshal."

"You're getting too damn free and easy. I left you cuffed to the stove last night, and what do I find this morning? A note telling me how you helped yourself to freedom without my by your leave. Now if you want to enter some kind of contest with me, I'll sure as hell put you straight in a hurry. To start with, you're gonna stay where I put you, or by God I'll fix you where you will."

Jody heard part of that speech at a distance as the marshal led Harry away. He stood rubbing his freed wrist, thinking about how to ask the marshal for something to eat. At last he decided he wouldn't ask, after all. He went first to give the animals fresh water, then he cleaned out the pens and buried the refuse. Next he sorted and buried the rest of the garbage. By that time it was mid-afternoon, and his hunger was simply a dull ache. Then it occurred to him that Harry hadn't had anything but a cup of coffee either.

That did it. He took a deep breath and went into the store where the marshal was leaned back in his chair, his feet up on the desk, the bandaged hand cradled carefully in the good one in his lap. A cigarette hung from the corner of his mouth, but it had gone out. He was asleep.

Jody sat down on a crate across the desk from him and waited. The marshal probably hadn't slept much the night before. After maybe five minutes, the eyelids flickered. Jody waited until he was fully awake. Soon the marshal coughed and shifted his weight in the chair. The fingers of the good hand closed around the wrist of the injured one, and the knuckles grew white. His eyes looked dully into Jody's eyes.

"It hurts a lot, huh?" Jody said.

The marshal studied him a minute. "Yeah," he said finally, "it sure does, kid."

"You want I should get you something? Maybe I could find Doc, and he might have some pain pills."

Slowly the marshal shook his head. "He'll likely be in after a while."

He's a proud man, Jody thought.

"Marshal, they's something we gotta do. Harry ain't had nothing to eat today, and—and I ain't either."

The marshal opened his eyes wide. "Oh hell, kid. I forgot all about it."

Jody relaxed a little. He had expected some kind of abuse.

Slowly the marshal took his feet from the desk. "They ain't nothing around here to eat." He reached for his billfold and pulled out a five dollar bill. "I guess you'll have to go over to Art's Cafe and see what you can find."

"I think it ain't open," Jody said. "Art and the whole family was at the funeral."

The marshal sat, the bill in his hand, looking uncertain. "Maybe I could get my wife to fix something."

Rose Becker came in the door, carrying a big cardboard box in both hands. She had walked all the way from her house, apparently, and she was sweating freely.

"'Lo, Marshal. 'Lo, Jody. The neighbors been bringing food by, more'n I'll ever eat afore it spoils with no icebox, so I brung some down fer Harry, and everyone else of course." She brought the box and set it on the desk.

Jody smelled baloney sandwiches and fried chicken. There was part of a cake and a bowl of potato salad.

"Hot damn, Rose," the Marshal said. "You sure come on cue. Harry and Jody ain't had no dinner." He looked at Jody. "Nor breakfast neither. We're much obliged."

Rose nodded, but she was already taking out some paper plates and some battered forks.

She looked better, Jody thought. She had brushed her hair out and put on some lipstick. She set the first plate before the marshal.

"Look, Rose, about them questions the other day—"

"Fergit it," Rose said. "I reckon you just done what you thought you had to." She looked at the bandaged hand he was holding up against his shoulder. "What'd you do to that hand?"

"I got dog bit," he said. "Doc sewed it up, but it smarts a little." He began on a piece of chicken.

Rose gave a plate to Jody. "You ought to take that hand home and soak it in some hot salt water," she said.

"Yeah, I might do that," he said around the chicken breast he was eating. Suddenly he stopped chewing and closed his eyes. The sweat popped out on his forehead.

"Go on home," Rose said. "What's the good of sitting around here hurting? Jody can watch things."

"Damned if I don't think I will," he said. He took his piece of chicken and a sandwich with him, leaving the plate with the potato salad on his desk, and slouched out the door. They heard his feet scuff on the gravel outside, the creak of the door of his truck, then a tinny slam. The motor started, and he drove away.

"You're not eating," Rose said.

"I'll wait on Harry and you," Jody said.

In Earthen Vessels

Rose smiled. She had filled another plate for Harry and one for herself, and they went into the garage.

"Dinnuh is suhved!" she announced.

Harry gave a laugh. "Boy, am I glad to see you. My stomach thinks my teeth has gone out of business."

Rose stood looking down into the pit. "My God, Harry, what a jail," she said softly. "I never realized how you was living over here."

"Shucks," Harry said, "it does lack some of the features often found in high–class jails, but then it's got some you–nique features of its own. Take the clientele, now, and the atmosphere."

Rose swallowed hard, but she hesitated only a moment. "Jody and me come to have a meal with you." She started down the steps.

"Wait, now, Rose," Harry said. "Don't come down here in this stink. Don't sit on them steps either. You'll get all dirty. Tell you what. I been working on this wire cage here, and you know I think I might be able to join you in the parlor." He pried up on the frame of the possum's cage until it came apart at the top. He slipped the cuff off the upright piece, then disentangled it from the chicken wire, which had been broken through. "See, you just keep bending this wire back and forth until it gets hot enough, and it comes right in two. Sorry, Possum ol' buddy, but I'm gonna leave you fer a while. I'll be back."

He rose stiffly, stretched his legs, then came up out of the pit. "Let's go in the office. It'll be more pleasant. Tell you what, I'm gonna wash my hands at the pump. I'll join you in a minute."

Rose and Jody carried the plates back into the office. Rose looked around, then set the plates on the top of the stove. "This can be our table," she said. She began to pull up a crate for a seat. Then she took hold of the judge's swivel chair where Bill had sat on Monday afternoon. Suddenly a confused look passed over her face, and she stood motionless, her hand resting on the back of the chair.

Jody put his plate down on the stove top beside the other two. "I'm real sorry, Mrs. Becker."

Rose shut her eyes and slumped over the chair. "Oh Bill, why?"

In a few seconds, she stood upright, resolutely picked up the chair, and set it down firmly near the stove. "Not a word, now," she said. She pulled up another crate and settled it in place as Harry came through the door.

"Please to be seated, Mr. Bewley," she said, turning the swivel chair toward him.

"Now ain't this grand," Harry said. "Jody, reach us three bottles of pop out of that box."

"I ain't got no money."

Harry looked at Rose and smiled. "Never mind that. I'll have the marshal put it on my bill."

Jody took three bottles out of the cool water, a strawberry pop for Rose, orange for himself, and cream soda for Harry. They all fell to with a good appetite.

"Now," Harry said to Jody as he started his second drumstick, "ain't you kind of glad the marshal forgot the cold oatmeal this morning?"

"Cold oatmeal?" Rose said in disbelief.

They all had a laugh, even though Jody wasn't sure why they were laughing.

They cleaned up the chicken and most of the sandwiches. Rose cut the cake into three large pieces, and they ate it all. At last Harry pushed the judge's chair back into its usual spot and sighed in contentment.

"Lovely, Rose. That puts me in good shape fer a serious talk."

Rose looked at Jody. "Oh, Harry, are you sure about this?"

"I'm sure. He's more a man than most men I've known. Let's ask him." He swiveled his chair toward Jody. "I need to tell you what Rose and me has decided to do. We can do it by ourselves if we have to, but we really need some help. I'm gonna ask you if you want to help us. You don't have to do it, and we won't think any less of you if you don't."

Jody sat very still. "Sure, Harry, whatever you–all need me to do."

"Don't promise nothing yet," Harry said. "It ain't nice, and I suspect it ain't quite legal. Hear us out first."

Harry stood up and looked out at the hot dusty street, much as he had done the first night he had slept there. "Seems to us that Bill Becker ain't had his just dues." He paused a long time. "Not that we can square everything fer him, but there's one thing we can do. We're gonna move him home."

Jody sat stunned. "What?"

Harry turned, sat down, and leaned over to look Jody right in the eyes. "We're gonna dig up that coffin and bring it here and bury Bill again in his own back yard. We're gonna do it tonight."

The room began to reel. Jody was suddenly out of his body again, floating at a great height, looking down on himself and Rose and Harry sitting around the stove.

"Are you all right?" Harry said.

Jody forced himself back. "Sure. Go on."

"That's about it. We're gonna take my truck and some shovels and a lantern, and dig him up. Then we're gonna bring him home and put him in more friendly earth before the Lord's sun dawns again."

Jody looked at Rose. There was a calm, a repose in her face that made her large features majestic. He felt a rush of awe. He was in the presence of something beyond his grasp, and yet he was at home with it. It resonated within him like a voice he knew well but had not heard for years. But he had to be sure. "Did you say it wasn't legal?"

Harry looked back at him steadily. "I said I didn't know. Maybe it is and maybe it ain't. Rose bought the plot where Bill is. She bought his coffin. She owns the land where we'll bury him. I reckon there's probably a way such things has got to be done, and likely this ain't the proper way, as the law thinks, but it's the way we're gonna do it. We don't want a lot of hullabaloo and papers to sign and fees to pay. Most of all we don't want the whole county coming around to gawk and laugh and sneer and offer opinion where it ain't been asked. This here's nobody's business but ours and Bill's. I'm bound to tell you, little buddy, that if we get caught we may be in a mess."

"I can see that," Jody said. He grinned a little. "Mr. Matthias would be upset."

There was a flicker of a grin on Harry's face, but he said nothing. They were waiting.

"I'm right honored you asked me," Jody said. "When do we start?"

Rose and Harry both burst into a short laugh. "Not yet," Harry said. "First off, you need to try to get some sleep this afternoon, if you can. We've got to get our equipment together. I don't quite know where some of it can be got, but we may need to get it in the dark."

"There's a shovel here," Jody said.

"And I got one, and a lantern," Rose said, "though it's gonna be moonlight."

"What we really need," said Harry, "is a hoist, or something to do the work of one. I don't know what we can do fer that."

"They's some old pulleys out behind the garage," Jody said. "We need some rope."

"That sounds likely. I'll take a look. Now, Rose, you take my truck and park it up by your place. If anybody asks, you've borried it fer a few days. Better get some gas. Here's some money fer it." He took three dollars from his worn billfold. "You go on now and try to sleep a bit yourself. We'll be up there after it's good and dark, about ten or so."

Rose gathered up the plates and forks and put the sandwiches back in the box.

"Take that food along, and we'll need some water," Harry said.

"See you later then," Rose said. Before she left, she came over and gave them both a hug, both at once. "I won't never fergit this." She picked up her box, took the keys to the truck, and was gone.

"Now I want you to sleep awhile, little buddy," Harry said. "It's gonna be a long hard night."

Jody threw his bedroll on the office floor, and though it was hot and his mind was in a whirl, he was soundly asleep almost at once.

Chapter Thirteen

When he woke it was nearly dusk. Slowly he realized Harry had him by the foot, shaking him gently. He sat up and instantly remembered everything. The smell of fresh coffee filled the office. Harry handed him a cup and picked up his own from the marshal's desk.

"Reckon I'll owe the marshal a pound of coffee when I quit boarding here," Harry said.

"Did you find them pulleys?"

"I did. I couldn't find no rope, and I didn't want to risk stirring around town looking fer some. I did find a length of tow–chain with a good hook on both ends. I cut some lengths of barbed wire from that roll hanging on the fence out back. Maybe we can make do." He paused and sipped. "One thing more. We need something to fill a hole. Rock would be okay, but I don't want to haul that much weight."

Jody thought a minute. "They's some old fence posts stacked down on the corner of the Jamison place."

"Just the thing," Harry said. "All else we need we've got, except maybe enough luck to get this job done without attracting any attention. It'd be pretty hard to explain why we're hauling a coffin around and me with this bracelet on."

Jody tried to laugh at that and not think how scared he was.

"You can still back out," Harry said.

"Not on your life," Jody said. He started pulling on his shoes.

"Well, to tell the truth, Rose and me would have a hard time doing this without you," Harry said with a grin. "We was gonna try anyway, but I ain't much good at real work anymore. I ain't got no strength. We can sure use a real man on this job."

Jody glowed inside. He couldn't think of anything to say, so he bent over his shoes, smiling to himself. It was a great feeling.

"It's dark," Harry said. "Let's go."

He took the roll of wire he had prepared over one shoulder and then gathered up the tow chain in his other hand. Jody locked the store, then picked up the shovel as he went out through the back door, propping it open so they could get back in. They went stealthily down the side of Art's Cafe, keeping to the shadows. They made their way to Rose's place without incident. They didn't go to the house, but straight to the truck where it was parked in front. Rose was already there, waiting for them.

They laid the wire and tools in the bed and got softly into the cab. Rose had the lantern propped between her feet and a box with some food and water on her lap. Harry took the truck out of gear and Jody pushed it enough to start it rolling before he jumped in. They rolled quietly down the long drive in the soft moonlight. Only when they were out on the empty road did Harry start the motor.

Instead of going back through town, Harry headed down a section line, skirting Trasherdell on the south, and then a mile beyond town they pulled up at the corner of the old Jamison place. There was a pile of split posts, about six feet long each, making a dark place in the moonlight. Jody felt his way through the barbed wire fence and tossed about twenty of the posts over the fence onto the right–of–way. Rose picked them up and put them in the truck bed, while Harry pushed them into place with his foot.

They got quietly back into the cab, and the truck, heavier now, turned back north until they intersected the highway.

"Is this as fast as we can go?" Rose said.

"It's as fast as we ought to go," said Harry. "We don't want old truck to overheat or anything, now do we? Easy does it, Rose old gal. Just remember, they ain't no reason fer this not to work."

"Sure, Harry. I can think of about twenty ways it could not work."

"One step at a time," Harry said. "The next thing is to get to the cemetery without breaking down."

They clattered along at about forty miles an hour, less on the hills, and met only a few vehicles. Once a carload of kids followed them for about a mile, but went by shouting jeers and left them quickly behind. At the south edge of Ashton, Harry turned off the

In Earthen Vessels

highway and drove to the cemetery the roundabout way past the old water tower. They drove up to the cemetery entrance, laboring on the long hill. Nobody seemed to be anywhere around.

"Here goes," Harry said, pulling in. "You–all check me out to make sure we're going the same track we took this morning."

"I'm no help," Rose said. "I didn't pay no attention."

"This is it," Jody said. "Take a left at the next lane and go till the gravel runs out."

Where the lane stopped, they could see the track of the funeral procession in the grass. Ahead, in the headlights, was a mound of red dirt.

Harry steered the truck out in a half–circle and backed up almost against the foot of the grave. He cut the motor and lights, and instantly the world was silent, except for the noise of the locusts all around.

They got out and closed the doors quietly. Harry set the lantern down inside the truck bed and lit it. It cast a dim light on the grave when they let down the tailgate, but it wouldn't be visible from any other direction.

They laid aside the judge's wreath of carnations, already wilted form the heat of the day, and Rose and Jody began shoveling the red dirt onto the stained place where the diggers had shoveled it before. Once they were down about eight inches, Harry took the lantern and set it down in the trench they were digging. They worked as quietly as they could and talked only in whispers. The soft orange glow of the kerosene lantern lit up their sweaty faces grotesquely, but the locusts sang on as if the scene here enacted were only a proper and ordinary ritual. Perhaps the creation was not going to take any special notice of them after all.

Little by little the trench deepened, as they moved the lantern from end to end out of their way. Slowly they burrowed down where Bill Becker waited for them patiently, more patient than they, more silent. At last they could hear the shovels making a different sound, the sound of something hollow under their feet.

"Careful, now," Rose said. "Don't scratch that purty box." She dropped to her knees and began scooping away the dirt with her hands. Jody also kneeled down to help. Under his fingers was a flat surface. He felt to the edge, then down beside it, and in the dry crumbly clay he found the long bar he and Harry had carried the casket by that morning.

"Here it is," he said, scooping away the dirt to show the edge of the casket and the metal bar beside it. In a few minutes they had scraped the dirt away to expose the top of the coffin and the carrying bars on both sides.

Harry let himself down into the trench beside them, two short lengths of the wire in his hand. He worked a wire around the bar near the head of the casket and then twisted the ends of it back into a crude knot around the wire. He turned to the other side and dug until he could work the wire around the other bar. With his pliers he twisted the knot tight. Then he did the same with the other length, twisting it around the first to strengthen it.

"Now comes the tricky part," Harry said. He lifted himself out of the hole, and Rose clambered out after him.

"Take your shovel and dig out a little around the head of that coffin," he told Jody. "It's got to have a little space to straighten up."

Jody stood on Bill's casket, just above his throat, and threw several more shovels of clay out of the hole. Then Harry dropped Jody the chain. Jody hooked it into the wire, handed up the lantern, and climbed out.

Harry stretched the tow chain the length of the grave and hooked it to the frame of his truck near the tailgate. Then he started the truck and eased it forward. Slowly, the casket stood upright in the grave. Jody had a sudden image of Bill Becker standing in his casket, arms folded across his chest.

Harry set the brake, took the truck out of gear, and got out, leaving it running. "Take them posts, the soundest of them, and make a cradle across the hole behind that coffin, but handle them careful. We don't want to leave a lot of bark and deadwood lying round the gravesite."

Jody got up in the truck bed and picked the four best posts. Then he and Rose laid them across the grave. Then while Harry backed the truck slowly, they stood on each side and lugged the casket as far as they could onto its cradle.

It was no use. The casket was too heavy for the two of them to lift enough to get it out of the hole.

"What'll we do?" Rose said. She sounded worried.

Harry swore quietly to himself, and then just sat for a minute or two.

"All right," he said at last. "Go ahead and put some more of them posts across the grave." He unhooked the chain from the truck. The casket leaned comfortably across the nearest post. After Rose and Jody built more cradle, he pulled the truck away, took it in a wide circle around to the head of the grave, and hooked back up to the truck.

Slowly, carefully, he eased the truck forward, tugging at the casket, the chain now stretched taut in the air between the truck and the wire sling at the top of Bill's casket. Slowly, with a grating sound, it came up out of the grave, scraping its bottom on the posts. Harry dragged it gently all across the cradle, out onto the grass.

As he killed the motor, a dog barked at a farmhouse less than a quarter–mile away. A pole light came on in a yard. Instantly Harry blew out the lantern, and they all stopped in their tracks. The dog kept barking. After what seemed a long time, a male voice spoke roughly, the dog quieted, and the light went out. "Okay," Harry whispered. "First we get them posts all out of the truck and into the hole. We put the casket in the truck, and we fill the grave. We gotta do all that in the dark."

Rose handed the posts down to Jody, who laid them noiselessly where the casket had been. Then they managed to get one end of the casket up onto the tailgate. Then the three of them hoisted the other end up and pushed the casket ever so slowly into the truck. Last, Rose and Jody shoveled the mound of dirt back into the hole, rounding it over the top until it looked as much as possible like a real grave. Meanwhile Harry carefully draped the chain through the handles of the casket and around the bed of the truck, hooking either end to the frame beneath.

"We been here too long," Harry said. "Let's get out of here."

"Wait," Jody said. He picked up the wreath and placed it atop the grave. Then they took a quick look around to be sure they had everything. They had a few moments of panic until they found the lantern.

Then Harry started the motor, and back over the dim path they went, easing their way in the moonlight. Once out of the cemetery, he turned the lights on. They again gave the town a wide berth. Harry drove on four miles of dirt road before he eased onto the highway again.

"So far, so good," Rose said.

"Yeah," Harry said. "They was a squeak or two, but we made it. Now if we can just get around Trasherdell without having to explain our cargo."

"Boy, wouldn't we of had a time, trying to do that without Jody?" Rose said.

"I don't want to think about it," Harry said.

"Likely we'd a wound up having to leave old Bill standing straight up in his grave," Rose laughed. "Wouldn't Mr. Matthias have been surprised."

They all laughed, relaxing a little from the strain.

"Pass around the sandwiches, Rose," Harry said. "Let's take a bit of nourishment. We still got a hard night's work to do."

They ate the sandwiches and had all they wanted to drink. Harry kept watching his rearview mirror. Soon they came to the corner north of Jamison's and turned off, reversing their route. Harry went a mile farther west and came to Rose's place from the side away from town. A hundred yards from the house he turned the pickup into the fallow field and came up on the backside of the Becker acreage.

"Say when, Rose," Harry said. "We don't want to get any closer to the house than necessary."

"Beyond that tree is our property line," Rose said.

Harry pulled up by the tree. Quietly they got out. The world was still and dark.

"Now this has got to be done careful," Harry said. He lit the lantern, cleared a spot in the tall grass with his hands, and set it down carefully.

"Wait," Rose said. "We sure don't want to start a fire." She took the rest of the water and poured out enough to soak the ground where the lantern sat.

Harry took the spade and cut the turf carefully in long, straight lines. Then he cut wedges of turf, about a foot square, and lifted each out tenderly, setting them along the outside of the plot he was preparing. Once that was done, Rose and Jody finished the hole, throwing the dirt into the truck bed alongside the casket. When the hole was about five feet deep, they muscled the casket into the hole, filled it on up with the loose earth to within three inches of the top, and set the wedges of turf back, each in its proper place.

At last, they breathed deep and relaxed. Harry blew out the lantern and loaded the tools. Then they all sat around Bill's new grave in the soft moonlight.

Rose and Harry talked softly about Bill, how generous he was, how kindly, how full of life and fun in the old wild days together. "You would of liked him, Jody, if you could of knowed him then," Harry said.

"He didn't mean you no harm by talking so harsh the other day," Rose said. "He just got that way slowlike, you know, over so many years. It got to where he couldn't laugh at nothing no more, and I couldn't do nothing that cheered him, seemed like. Then people kind of stayed away from us. I can understand that. Bill got to where he didn't want to see nobody neither. You got to forgive him, Jody. He just wasn't his old self anymore, and he didn't even know what he was doing sometimes."

"Sure," Jody said. "I understand."

"You know, I think you really do." Rose was crying softly again, but it was all right this time, Jody could tell.

They were silent for a time.

"Jody, son, I seen you praying the other night," Harry said. "I know you're a godly man. Could you say a few words over Bill, maybe? It would help."

Jody's heart sank. He thought how he had been an intruder upon Bill's last bitter hours, how he would bring more anguish to Rose someday when he must share his grim secret, how by his default the marshal had been confused and misled, how the miserable imprisonment Harry had endured was really his doing because of it.

"I ain't," he blurted out. "I ain't godly, and I ain't a man." The whole confession was pushing to escape his mouth. He stopped and swallowed it back. To spoil this moment for Rose and Harry because of his own selfish need for the relief of confession would be another default. He couldn't do that. Sadly, he took up his burden of hypocrisy.

"I'll try," he said, and inwardly he prayed, *God forgive my lies.* How could he be forgiven when he was going to go ahead and be a fraud anyway? With an effort, he put the question away. Instead, he began to recite, from the scriptures he had read and heard from his childhood up.

"Let not your heart be troubled, neither let it be afraid," he began, and recited the whole passage down to "I am the way, the truth, and the life." The Twenty–third Psalm came, and then other passages, crowding one after another, and he let them speak. As their words moved him he wished deeply for peace for Rose and Harry, and the wish was making itself prayer before he realized it. A great rush of prayer for Bill came to him, until it would come out. He laid a hand on Rose's arm and one on Harry's and said simply, "Lord, forgive us all fer our wrong, and forgive Bill Becker every way he offended, and gather him into your care fer your mercy's sake only."

Before he felt the great rush of shame at his blasphemy, Rose Becker was squeezing his hand. He felt also the dangling cuff down his backbone as Harry's hand pressed his shoulder, and it was done, and he was a cheat and a fraud forever.

"One more little job for us, Buddy," Harry said as they stood and prepared to go. On a country road nearby they quickly shoveled the excess dirt from Bill's new grave into a ditch. They let Rose out at her gate and helped her collect her things from the truck. Then they went back to the store.

They drove up the back way and parked quietly at the back of the garage and let themselves in through the back door. Once more Jody felt his way around the wall to the light switch. They went into the office together, joking quietly about how tired they were, and Jody flicked on the light.

The marshal sat at his desk, a cigarette in his wounded hand, looking at them.

Chapter Fourteen

They stood motionless. Jody's mind raced. What did he know? What was he going to do? Had they been saying anything about the burial that he could have overheard?

"Welcome home," the marshal said humourlessly.

"Marshal! What air you doing up running around this hour of the night?" Harry said. His voice was steady, but his eyes were wild.

"I couldn't sleep with this hand. What's your excuse?"

"Well, looks like I'm caught fair and square. Ain't it just my luck? Some fellers get away with all kinds of mischief, and I can't get away with nothing. I sez to Jody, Hey, let's go down to my shack and see if we can find something to eat. So we been down there rummaging around—"

"No, you ain't. 'Cause I just been down there looking for you."

There was dead silence for nearly a minute. Jody kept quiet, out of the way. He figured his turn would come.

At last Harry sat down, facing the marshal across the desk. "No, I ain't. You're right."

"Would you like to try another story?"

"What's the difference?" Harry said. "Maybe I was wanting to get out of that hot, smelly hole fer a while, out into some clean air. Maybe I wanted a drink, and we went looking fer a bottle I hid when I was boozing it up in the old days. Maybe—"

"Maybe you was up to Rose Becker's place," the marshal said. He let the words sink in while he took a drag on his cigarette. Then he took the stub with his good hand, snuffed it out on the top of his desk, and flipped it into the trash barrel in the corner. "Your truck was at her place this afternoon about four. Now you come driving it in here."

Harry leaned back, his lips set. "Look, it don't make no difference where I been, and I don't think it's any of your business. Any-ways, I ain't telling you nothing about it."

"Okay," the Marshal said, rising slowly, "so that's the way it's gonna be. Back to the hole you go. This time you ain't going nowheres." He took the padlock from the latch inside the front door. Then he took down the light chain he had once used to beat Rupe. "Come on."

Harry rose resolutely. He followed him into the garage and down into the pit. Jody came to the door and watched.

"Sit," the marshal said.

Harry sat down in his accustomed spot. The marshal ran the chain in and out through the cages, threading it back and forth, but making all the loops come back to his hand. At last he took the padlock and clipped it through the two ends of the chain. Then he closed the open handcuff around the four or five loops of the chain he held in his hand. Harry was chained to all the cages across the end and corner of the pit.

"Now, by God," the marshal said, "there's more to keep you in your place than just your own respect fer the law. Next time you come out of that pit, it'll be because I unlocked them cuffs and no other reason."

Harry screwed up his face like he was going to answer, but then looked at Jody, clamped his mouth shut, and turned his head away. The marshal trudged up out of the pit, holding his bandaged hand. He walked straight up to Jody, who retreated into the office and sat down in the corner, his feet pulled under him. The marshal stood looking at him.

"Now," he said to Jody, "I want to know what's going on."

Jody's heart thumped, but he said nothing.

"All right," the marshal said, after a minute, "I'm too damned tired and sore to mess with you tonight, but I've got a piece of advice fer you, lad. You keep on making like Harry Bewley, and you're gonna do a stretch in prison someday." He took a turn up and down the room, holding his bandaged hand in front of him like a placard.

"You better sleep fast, if you're going to, 'cause I'll be here at sunup. We're gonna run that route, and I'm gonna keep a close eye on you from now on. One more wrong turn, and you go back to the farm, you hear me?"

"Yes sir," Jody said, not very loud.

The marshal walked around and around the stove, looking at Jody hard, watching for some sign of overt rebellion. Jody cowered and kept his face straight. At the same time, there was a little seed of delight in his heart. The marshal couldn't make him talk, and the marshal knew it.

Pretty soon he stopped pacing, picked up his hat from the desk, and walked out. The truck started up and pulled away.

Immediately Jody got up and went to see about Harry. The marshal had left the light on, and the birds and animals in their cages were stirring restlessly. Harry sat leaning against the empty cage where the owl had been, his head thrown back, eyes closed, throat uplifted and exposed.

"Are you all right?" Jody said. In place of the exhilaration of the evening, he felt disquieted.

"Sure," Harry said, not opening his eyes. "Everything's fine. I'm back home here with my friends,"

"He don't know nothing," Jody said, coming to sit on the steps.

Harry took a minute to answer. "He knows there's something, but he don't know what it is."

"He won't find out from me."

Harry opened his eyes. "You're okay, kid. Still, he's probably right, you know. Follow me around, I'll lead you wrong."

"If I go wrong," Jody said, "it'll be my own doing, nobody else's."

Harry grinned. "Well, that's a load off my mind. Still, you may of noticed, fer what it's worth, that my line of conduct sometimes gets me in trouble."

"Getting in trouble ain't the same as going wrong."

Harry looked at him. "That there can be a costly philosophy, little buddy. You go on believing that, and the world is gonna try to whip it out of you. The folks with the whip can't stand fer that to be true." He was smiling. He leaned his head back against the cage. "I can see right now, ain't no point talking to you. You're done ruint, and you ain't never gonna have no luck or easy times your whole life through."

"Yep," Jody said, "I'm a lost cause." The seed inside sprouted, put out leaves, bloomed. It was going to be okay, and Harry was all right. "We gonna sit around and swap compliments all night, or we gonna get some sleep? You want a drink of water afore I tuck you in?"

"Nah," Harry said, "give one a drink, and all the animals will want one. Let's pack it in."

"You want I should turn out the light?"

"Sure. Possum and me will sleep better if we don't have to look at one another."

"See you in the morning, then," Jody said, getting up. He turned off the light, and the pit sank into a deep, dark hole.

"Jody," Harry said out of the black, "thanks fer everything."

He didn't trust himself to answer. He took off his shoes, shook out the bedroll, and turned out his light. He sat down on the pallet and thought back through the long, long day. Afterward he prayed, in a whisper, for a long time.

He slept fitfully. Images of the night's experiences were woven into complex fantasies. In one dream they were all in Ashton cemetery. Rose had spread a meal of sandwiches and potato salad around the lantern, though it was broad daylight. Harry was there, Bill Becker, Mrs. Gamble, the judge, and an old man in a uniform with a medal. As they were about to eat Mr. Matthias stood bolt upright in a nearby grave and said, "No, we haven't said grace yet." That made the old soldier mad, and he said, "Shut up, boy." When Jody looked around he saw that the cemetery stretched all the way to the horizon in every direction, and all the gravestones were glistening in the sunlight.

In another dream, he was home on the farm, waking up in the cool early morning in his bed with the smell of buttered bread toasting in the oven and his mother singing at her work in the kitchen. Dad was saying they would go dig that field of sweet potatoes this morning before it got too hot to work. He was getting out of bed when he thought the animals hadn't had any water. He said, "Dad, I got to take care of them first." When he went out to the cages, they were all sick. Rupe said, "You're too late, Jody. The owl is dead." He went to see about the owl and there was Harry all doubled and crammed into the owl's cage.

There were several more dreams. In his last dream right before morning, he was back at the Animal Store, sweeping the office, and Johnny was telling a story about a circus and how the circus owner was going to breed a tiger with a hippopotamus, but the tiger wouldn't go into the water and the hippo wouldn't come out. While everybody was laughing at Johnny's story, Mr. Justice pulled up outside. He came in the door and said, "Is Mr. Matthias here?" They all stopped laughing but finally Johnny said, with a wink to everybody, "I'm Mr. Matthias. What do you want?" Mr. Justice said, "I've got somebody here I want you to board at the Trasherdell Kennels," and he brought in the marshal on a leash. The marshal had one forepaw all bloody, and he carried it curled up in front of him. Mr. Justice brought him over to Jody and said, "Don't let him get a mange," and Jody said he wouldn't. Mr. Justice said to the marshal, "Say Hello and shake hands," and the marshal stuck out the mangled forepaw to Jody. He didn't want to take the paw because it was bloody, but everybody was watching. The marshal was looking straight at him and holding out the paw, so he reached out and took hold of it. It was as hard and cold as ice. He woke with a start, his hand resting on the iron stove leg.

He sat up. His head felt heavy, and he was still tired. He was too disturbed by his dreams to try to sleep again. Besides, there was a little gloom of daylight in the room. He put on his shoes and got to his feet stiffly. He washed his face at the pump. Though it was barely light, he took the bucket and made his rounds, except he didn't go into the pit where Harry was still asleep.

He sat down by Rupe's cage and talked to him softly, trying to make his bad feelings go away. The sky got lighter. Before it was dawn, he was back inside, waiting for the marshal.

He didn't have long to wait. The marshal came in sullen and pale. There was a clean bandage on his hand. He went immediately to the pit to look at Harry. Satisfied his prisoner was secure, he said to Jody, "Let's go." He hadn't brought anything for Jody or Harry to eat.

Jody said nothing about it. He went at once to load the green drums into the marshal's truck and wired them securely in their places. The marshal was already sitting in the cab, a cigarette held in the fingers of his bandaged hand. Jody banged on the cab top to signal he was ready to go. The marshal took time to light the cigarette. He started the truck and took off faster than usual. Jody had to grab hold to keep his balance.

All the time he was emptying up the refuse, the Marshal kept racing the motor, hurrying him along. He drove fast and rough from stop to stop. Jody couldn't keep from getting flustered and angry, but he hurried through his work as best he could. As they raced through Trasherdell, the marshal took a corner too close and fast, and swiped a telephone pole. The jolt knocked Jody's feet from under him and he sat down hard in the truck bed. The marshal stopped, got out, slammed the door, and stood looking at the long rumpled place in his truck bed.

"Goddamn pole!" the marshal shouted.

Suddenly Jody laughed. He couldn't help it, it simply came out. He sat in the bed of the old truck, among the garbage drums, his buttocks still tingling from the jolt, and laughed uncontrollably.

The marshal looked at him, jaw set. He began walking around the truck, just as he had walked around the stove last night, kicking at the tires. Finally he stopped and looked at Jody until Jody stopped laughing.

"Ain't that just funny as hell," he said.

"Well," Jody said, "why'd you tear around town like a hot-rodder if you don't want to bang up your truck?" He was amazed at himself, but he didn't care. He was surprised to find out he wasn't afraid of the marshal anymore. The feeling was intoxicating.

"What's that to you?" the marshal said. "What's got into you, anyhow? You think you're smart, that's what, running round with Harry Bewley all night, you little fart. You just load that garbage."

"Aye, aye, Cap'n," Jody said, with a grin. "We gotta finish this run, so's I can hurry back and sweep."

The marshal stared at him in disbelief. Finally he spat deliberately and turned to get in the cab. "Smartass kid," he said to nobody in particular.

They finished the route at a somewhat slower pace. Back at the store, without speaking to him again, the Marshal went into the office, where Johnny Burton and Doc had already made up the first pot of coffee.

Jody fed the animals and took water to those in the pit. Then he sat down with Harry for a while. Harry was dirty, his clothes rumpled, the stubble of his beard making his face look rough. There were dark circles under his eyes.

"Little buddy," he said, "are we gonna get anything to eat today, do you suppose?"

"Marshal didn't bring nothing," Jody said.

"Well," Harry said, "would you see if one of them fellers in there would pour me a cup of that coffee. It sure smells good."

Jody rose and went into the office. Doc had the bandage off the marshal's hand and was swabbing at the reddened scar.

"Looks awful," the marshal said.

"Never mind that," Doc said. "It's healing just fine. It won't look pretty, but it'll be all right in a few days. Just keep it clean."

"Harry says he'd like a cup of that coffee," Jody said. He looked at the marshal, but he spoke to everybody.

Johnny was sitting by the pot. "Sure thing," he said, and grabbed one of the chipped cups. The marshal had been getting ready to say something, but he kept quiet as Johnny poured the coffee and handed it to Jody. Without looking at the marshal again, Jody turned quickly and took the coffee to Harry. Johnny followed him into the garage.

"Looks like the marshal's got you hog–tied good and tight this time," Johnny said.

"Yeah," Harry said, taking the cup. "Well, you see, I been a bad boy."

Johnny came over and sat down on the edge of the pit. He didn't laugh at Harry's little joke. "Would you like a smoke?"

"That'd be nice," Harry said, "only I'd have to ask you to roll it fer me. I never did learn to do it with one hand, like that Randolph Scott feller in the movies."

Johnny took out his tin of Prince Albert and the packet of papers, separated one, and filled it expertly from the tin.

"Tell me one thing straight, Harry," he said. "Did you cut Bill Becker's throat?"

"Johnny," Harry said, patiently, "you listen to too many stories. You've knowed me ever since you was in your teens. Hell, you ought to know I didn't. Bill was my friend."

"You was in love with Rose once," Johnny said. He climbed down the steps and handed him the cigarette. "If I understand what happened in there the other day, you're still in love with her." He struck a match.

Harry put the cigarette between his lips and dragged on it while Johnny held the light for him. Then he looked Johnny straight in the eyes. "Because I love Rose is all the more reason I couldn't have hurt Bill."

Johnny blew out the match slowly. At last he dropped his eyes. "You weren't jealous?"

"A long time ago I was near out of my mind, I was so jealous. A man grows out of that, you know."

There was a long silence. Jody sat on the steps and watched the two men. At last, when it seemed neither would ever say anything, Jody said, "How?"

Harry looked at him. Johnny raised his head and looked at Harry.

"Time," Harry said, "and grief. Time and grief enough will cure most anything. It's downright amazing what a man can learn with grief fer a teacher."

The judge's round figure came through the office doorway, his cup in his hand. He studied the scene before him gravely. Jody saw his eye following the chain where it threaded its way in and out through the mesh of the cages, coming back after each loop to pass again through the handcuff.

"Marshal," the judge said, without speaking to the three people in the pit, "what kind of rig is this? Did you ever hear the phrase 'cruel and unusual punishment'?"

The marshal came into the garage, his hand newly bandaged, with Doc behind him.

"That man won't stay put," he said to the judge. "I tried to be easy on him, and he just kept letting hisself out, running around all over town at his own discretion. I had to fix him so's he'd be where I could find him."

"See here, man, you can't treat him like one of your animals. Even a man under arrest is entitled to food and privacy."

"We been through all that already," the marshal said. "If y'all are so all-fired anxious to take care of lawbreakers, why don't you build me a proper jail? If you want a prisoner fed, how about the citizens of Trasherdell paying fer it?" He defiantly looked around at everyone, then came back to the judge. "You're pretty high and mighty when it don't cost nothing. Maybe one of you would like to have this damn job."

"Hey, hold on," the judge said, holding up his hand. "Nobody wants your job, and nobody expects you to do what you can't do. But you have to abide by the law too, like anybody else." He walked over to the marshal and began to talk to him earnestly. "Now, number one, you can't hold a prisoner indefinitely without cause. Either file your charges against him or let him go. Number two, if he's charged and held, he has a right to humane treatment. It's your responsibility to see, somehow, that he's treated humanely."

It was no use. The marshal set his jaw and looked at the floor.

The judge stopped, clearly aware he was not making any progress.

"You ain't no judge, and I ain't in court," the marshal said. "You're just another private citizen. I'm gonna be marshal, by God, as long as I'm marshal, not you and not Sheriff Lonnie and not Harry Bewley by a damn sight."

"Excuse me," Harry said, "but I'd like to make a point. First, I'm hungry. Second, I'm real interested in cooperating with the marshal any way he says. Third, I'd like to get on with this. If I'm gonna be tried, I'm ready to do it tomorrow, or sooner if possible. So what do you say, Marshal? Can we start with some breakfast? I'd be glad to buy my own."

"Don't order me around!" the marshal shouted.

The concrete surfaces of the garage rang with his voice. Everyone looked at one another. Then Johnny boosted himself up out of the pit and sat down on the edge. Then the judge sat down, and finally Doc. Jody was still sitting on the steps. The marshal walked slowly around the pit, not looking at anyone, while they all waited.

"Jody," the marshal said, finally, taking his billfold from his pocket and taking out a bill, "take this five dollars over to Art and tell him I want five dollars worth of breakfast. Hotcakes, bacon, eggs, whatever he's got. I want the whole five worth, and you, smart man," he pointed to Harry, "are gonna eat it all. Every crumb."

He threw the bill at Jody and stalked out into the office. Nobody moved. They could hear him in the office. "Marge, get me the sheriff." After a moment, he continued. "Sheriff, this is the marshal of Trasherdell. I got a man here I want charged with murder. Would you please, sir, at your convenience, come pick him up." The receiver banged down loud.

Jody rose and stole out of the back door past Harry's truck, and made his way somberly to Art's Cafe. He put the five dollars on the counter and told Art what he wanted.

Art shook his head. "That's a lot of breakfast," he said. He set to work. He broke a dozen eggs in a bowl while half a pound of bacon and six sausage patties sizzled on the grill. Meanwhile his daughter

Sally buttered and toasted a loaf of bread. Jody sat in an empty booth, drawing the aroma of the bacon into his nostrils and watching, with interest, the motions of Sally's shoulders and back. Once she turned quickly and caught him staring at her. He felt the blood rise through his face, and, mortified, knew she could see his blush through the summer tan. He dropped his eyes at once, but when he stole another glance he saw she was smiling to herself.

"Jody, don't you want something to eat?" Art said.

"No, thanks."

"You might as well have some of this. Harry can't eat all of it."

"It ain't fer me. Leastwise I don't know that it is. The marshal ordered it fer his prisoner."

"I see," Art said. He poured out a big glass of milk and took two sweet rolls from the case, and set the milk and rolls before Jody. "On the house," he said. "That's for bringing me all this business."

Jody thanked him and surrendered himself to the rich delight of the rolls. It wasn't too many times lately he'd had a breakfast like that. He looked up once and saw Sally watching him eat. Now it was her time to blush. Well, he thought, it's because she's curious about why I'm so hungry. The sight of her face turning slowly pink and the quiet brown eyes stayed in his memory like the fragrance of roses in a room.

He came in the back way to find Harry alone in the garage. Everyone else had gone back to the office to sit around the stove. He took the big platter of food down into the pit to Harry. It was good to see Harry's eyes light up, though he shook his head in disbelief. Jody left him to eat by himself and turned back to his morning's work. He knew Harry would ask him to eat some of the meal, and he didn't know how to respond. One thing for sure, the marshal didn't need anything else to set him off on another rampage, and Jody didn't think it would please the marshal for Harry to share his food.

For a moment he couldn't find the shovel to bury the garbage. With a start he remembered it was in the truck. When he went to get it he looked around him nervously, but the marshal and all the others were talking and laughing in the office and so nobody noticed. He thought also about moving the tow chain, but that would make a noise if he wasn't careful, so he left it in the truck.

After he had finished his work, he slipped into the back of the office and picked up his broom and began sweeping. The men in the room, as usual, paid him little attention.

"Well," Johnny was saying, "I reckon Mr. Justice won't come back, and we won't hear no more from him. I reckon you got you a fine stud in that chow, Marshal."

"Remember, Marshal, you owe me," Doc said. "I'm going to bring that bitch down here and get her bred."

"Reckon I'll have to spruce him up a bit," the marshal said. "Ain't nothing wrong with that dog, but you know how them fancy folks are. They want to see the papers and check the pedigree and all. If a dog ain't been brushed and manicured, they think he can't be a good stud. Damned if I can see what a dog's toenails has to do with siring pups."

Johnny laughed. "I ain't never seen one use his toenails." Everybody laughed.

"Well, if they want purty toenails, I reckon it can be arranged," the marshal said. "I'll tell y'all one thing, I'm gonna put a muzzle on that chow afore I try to paint his toes."

"Better let Jody put the muzzle on," Doc said. "That dog doesn't seem to like you."

"You're going to be busy, Marshal, if you open up another business on the side," the judge said.

The marshal spat tobacco juice deliberately into the bucket. "If old Rupe works out, I might just get two or three more good studs and do that business full time. A man can't be out gathering up garbage when them fancy city folks are bringing their cutsie–pie little bitches to be bred. I may have to clean this joint up a little and wear nice clothes, like a proper businessman."

"You might have to get yourself all manicured whilst you're prettying up old Rupe," Johnny said. "Derned if it won't be harder to make you presentable than that dog."

"What I'll have to do, smartass, is chase this gang of riffraff out of my office. No wonder I didn't get no respect from Mr. Justice. Soon as he looked at this clientele he decided right off my business must be shady." The marshal was grinning at his joke amid hoots of mock protest.

"Now Marshal," said the judge, "you know you'd be downright lonesome without your friends. Like right now, for instance. It's plumb empty in here without old Harry sitting in his place. Why don't you bring him in and let him have a smoke with us?"

The marshal's face hardened. "Nothing doing. Harry's gonna stay right where he is till the sheriff takes him off my hands. That guy's slippery as a weasel. I don't trust him."

Everyone sat in silence, awkwardly. The judge shook his head.

"You know, Marshal," Johnny said, finally, "maybe we've done Harry a wrong. You seen how Bill Becker was acting in here Monday afternoon. Maybe the sheriff's right. Maybe he did hisself in, and Harry didn't have anything to do with it."

"Well, when you're marshal, Johnny Burton, if you feel that way, you can do what you please. I'm telling you, there's more to Harry Bewley than meets the eye. There's something not right about that feller. Okay, say maybe I can't prove he's guilty, yet. Still, if everything don't seem right, and I let him go just because we been friends fer years, what kind of lawman does that make me?"

"But hell, Marshal—"

"Back off, Johnny. You too, Judge, Doc, all of you. One of these days, reckon I'll turn in this badge, and then see if there's anybody else in Trasherdell wants to try to do this damn job fer the pay. In the meantime, we're gonna do this my way."

They all let it drop. They made another pot of coffee about noon, and the judge sent Jody over to Art's again to buy hamburgers for everybody, Jody too, and paid for it himself. They had a regular picnic around the cold stove, just as Harry and Jody and Rose had done yesterday, and joked and chatted. From time to time Harry's name came up, or one of them would drop out of the group and go talk with Harry for a while. Jody checked on him often, emptied his can, spent a long midafternoon talk with him. The marshal never went to check on his prisoner again, and nobody ventured to talk about Harry's being freed.

In the late afternoon, about four, Johnny was telling an involved story about a Mississippi gambler. It seems he got a batch of girls and a madam together and was taking them west on the train all shut up secretly in their own coach, when Jesse and Frank James and Cole Younger held up the train. At that point, the sheriff's car pulled up outside and the sheriff came in, and suddenly nobody was interested in Johnny's story anymore.

"Well," said the marshal, "look who's finally here."

In Earthen Vessels

The sheriff sat down wearily on Harry's crate. "Let's get this done. Do you have any further evidence?"

The marshal eyed him evenly. "Last night Harry Bewley broke loose from where I secured him, and in the company of my employee Jody, absented hisself until two in the morning. They was doing something suspicious, but I don't know what."

"How is that related to the death of Bill Becker?"

"Damned if I know, but it is."

The sheriff rose and walked to the door of the garage. "Harry, where'd you go last night?"

"Begging your pardon, Lonnie, I ain't gonna tell you that. It didn't have a thing in the world to do with how Bill died."

The Sheriff studied Harry closely, then turned to Jody. "Well, son, is that true?"

"Yes," Jody said.

The sheriff returned to his seat. "Marshal, I'll put it to you straight. Bill Becker's death has been listed as a suicide. I've talked the case over with the county attorney and given him your oral report. He's reviewed the coroner's report also. He concludes you don't have a case and the prisoner should be freed."

The marshal looked at him hard, a red blush slowly rising on the back of his neck. "Well, that's a mistake. I ain't gonna let him go till I get to the bottom of this. You and your county attorney can do what you want."

The sheriff sighed. "I've spent all the time on you I can afford, Marshal. Either you let that man go, or I'll be back in the morning with a writ. I'm on my way to the city to pick up a prisoner, or I'd go get it now."

"Well, you'll just have to get your damned writ," said the marshal, red–faced. "And then the whole thing'll be on your head. As fer me, I'm not gonna be the one to let a suspected killer walk free. I might want to run fer sheriff sometime, and I don't want a blunder like that on my record."

"I'll see you in the morning, then," said the sheriff, matter–of–factly. He walked to the door of the garage and called to Harry.

"You hear me, Harry? Now sit tight and don't do anything stupid." He gave a glance at Jody, another at the judge, put on his hat and went out. Everybody sat listening to his car pulling away.

"Well, holy shit!" said the marshal, in a rage. "That tears it. When that bastard comes back in the morning, boys, I'm turning in my badge. What the hell's the use?" He stormed out of the office, climbed in his truck, and was gone.

Everyone went in where Harry sat and congratulated him and said how good it was all this was about to be over. They joked about who would take the job if the marshal really did turn in his badge. Finally the crowd broke up, and Jody and Harry were left to themselves.

They hashed it all over again while Harry fed the rest of the cold scrambled eggs to the birds and animals around him. About five–thirty Rose came in, bringing some cake and some tea to drink. They ate together in the pit this time, over Harry's protest. Rose brought one of the chairs from the office and sat right down in the pit with Harry. They told her what the sheriff had said.

"Tomorrow about this time," Harry said, "I'm gonna be out of here for good. After tonight, I ain't gonna sleep with a possum again as long as I live."

They laughed and joked about that, and talked quietly about what they had done the night before. Rose told them she had gone out to Bill's new grave in the morning and carried water for the sod they had replaced. Then she had a long, long talk with Bill. At last she said she would go for now, but would be back in the morning to take Harry home to breakfast when the sheriff turned him free. She went over to Harry and got down on her knees so she could embrace him and kiss him. Jody left them together and went out, happy and confused, and talked to Rupe.

When he returned, Rose had gone and Harry sat placidly among the cages, smiling to himself. Jody picked up the chair Rose had left, carried it back to the office, and set it down in its place. Afterward he and Harry talked until nearly dark, but they were both so tired from missing sleep the night before that they yawned and yawned, and decided at last to turn in early. Jody made one more round with his water bucket. When he came back, Harry was already slumped in a doze. He went at once to make out his pallet.

He had barely unrolled it and spread it out when he heard a familiar clatter as the marshal's truck pulled up outside. The doors of the truck both slammed. The voices of the marshal and Johnny came to Jody loud and slurred. The marshal pushed the door open roughly, and both of them walked in a little unsteady on their feet. The marshal had a nearly empty fifth of Old Crow in his good hand, and Johnny had another fifth, unopened.

The marshal had changed clothes. He was wearing a clean white shirt, a pair of dark dress slacks, and his new cowboy boots. He had put some pomade on his hair and slicked it down flat. He made his way to the desk, set the whiskey down carefully, and with his other hand, held up his badge for Jody to see. After Jody had stared at him for a while, the marshal opened the drawer of his desk and ceremonially put the badge in it.

"Afore witnesses," he said heavily. "You're my witness, I ain't drinking on duty. Tonight is my night off. What I do on my own time is nobody else's business."

"Nobody's business" Johnny said. He was not quite as far along as the marshal.

Jody was a little scared. "What are you gonna do?" he asked.

"Why, nothing illegal, son. Drinking whiskey ain't illegal in Oklahoma, just selling it is. Old Johnny and me is gonna have a few drinks together to celebrate my coming retirement. We might play a little blackjack, a friendly game, you know, and we might sing a song or two if we feel like it. Then we're gonna go home." He leaned over and glared at Jody. "Is that all right with you?"

Jody didn't say anything. He hadn't ever seen anybody drunk before, and he didn't know how to act.

"Is that all right with you, Mr. Bewley?" the marshal shouted, turning his head toward the garage.

"It's your party, Marshal," Harry said out of the pit.

"You're damn right it is," the marshal said.

"Hey, Harry," Johnny called, "Do you want a drink? We got some good stuff from the city boys, none of that rotgut you and Bill used to sell."

"No more fer me, boys, thanks," Harry said amiably. "I ain't man enough to handle it anymore."

The marshal sat down heavily at his desk. He started to take a drink from his bottle, then instead took a coffee cup and poured himself about half a cupful. He held up the bottle and looked at it. There was a little left in the corner. He tipped the bottle and emptied it into his cup.

"Hey, Johnny," he said, "you'll have to open the other'n. Pour it out in a cup, shithead. Don't drink out of the bottle. It ain't refined. We're gonna be refined around here from now on." He threw the empty bottle with deadly aim into the trash barrel in the corner with such force that it shattered.

Johnny sat down across the desk from the marshal, opened the second fifth, and poured himself nearly a cupful from the bottle. He took his can of Prince Albert from his hip pocket and a packet of papers from his shirt pocket. Suddenly he stopped as though he remembered something, and held up a finger. "Special treat fer your party, Marshal," he said, reaching in his other shirt pocket. "Store–bought smokes." He took out a pack of Camels, opened it, and offered it to the marshal. "I should of got some cigars."

"Them Camels is fine," the marshal said. "We'll have a cigar tomorrow on me after I tell the sheriff where to put that badge."

Johnny snorted. "I want to hear that. Peradventure the sheriff won't do it exactly the way he's instructed."

The marshal guffawed. "Peradventure! Where in hell did you learn to talk like that?"

"You said I was to be refined," Johnny said. "If you're gonna be refined, you gotta learn to talk like that, instead of calling your friends shithead."

The Marshal guffawed again, doubling over the desk. Johnny lit the cigarettes, laughing at his own joke, and handed one to the marshal. The marshal took it and dragged heavily on it, still chuckling in his throat. He stopped laughing and his face went ugly.

"Ten fucking years I been wearing that badge, and here comes this smart sheriff telling me what I can do and what I can't do. He thinks he's got me in a cage, and all he has to do is say shit and I'll say, how long? Well he can have it all, starting tomorrow, and see how he likes that. I ain't gonna try to hold the law together all by myself, and I ain't gonna be nobody's darky."

"Tell you what," said Johnny, taking out a deck of cards, "let's fergit Sheriff What's–His–Name and play a little blackjack. What's your stakes?"

"Up to you," said the Marshal, taking up his drink.

"Tell you what," Johnny said. "Whoever wins a hand gets a drink, and the other ain't allowed to. When we run out of whiskey, the game's over."

They started a noisy game, swearing and yelling amiably at one another. Jody watched for a while, then stole away to talk to Harry.

"I don't like this," he said.

"Does he have his gun?" Harry said.

"No."

Harry's face relaxed. "Don't let it bother you, little buddy. It don't mean nothing. The marshal is only taking the edge off his humiliation. Johnny is trying to be loyal to his friend. Worst thing'll happen is they'll feel all wrung out in the morning. That'll probably make tomorrow easier fer all of us. Tell you what, they's apt to get noisier afore they pass out, and maybe you'd be more likely not to get abused if you left them to themselves. I suggest you quietly drag your pallet out of there and sleep in here tonight."

Jody thought that was a good idea. Carefully he slipped back into the room and took his bed by the corner. They didn't even know he was gone. He threw the pallet alongside the pit and lay down, as tired as he had ever been in his life. He didn't even take off his shoes. For a time the light from the office and the voices of the two men kept sleep away. Finally all that was slowly drowned in his misery and fatigue, and he dropped into sleep.

Chapter Fifteen

In his dream he was at home in the bed he shared with his brother Tommy, only he was alone in the bed because it was the time years ago when he had been deathly sick. He relived the numbing fever and the sense of detachment from his own body. He recognized again in his dream that he was very ill. His hands groped over the cool iron of the bedstead with its distinct corners and curves. It was night, late night, in his dream, that hot dry August night when he had drifted in and out of delirium. There was his father beside him, handing him a dipper of cool water. It was not the murky creek water they had to drink after the well dried up, but fresh, cool delicious spring water, a whole bucket of it, that his father had fetched in the dead of the night for him, from who knows how far. He drank the cool, blessed water so gratefully there was nothing left of his thanks but the very act of drink.

He reached out, took his father's hand, and said, "Am I gonna die?"

His father, with only a little hesitation, said, "I don't know, son."

And there it was, naked and real, a dark thing in the room with them, standing with arms folded somewhere in a corner, Death. It waited noiselessly while Jody took another dipper of cool water in his hands.

All was just as he remembered it, and so he knew he was dreaming, living it over again. The next part, though, was new, not the way he remembered. Because his father said to the dark angel standing in the corner, "Not yet." Then he turned to Jody and said, "Son, you've got to get up and take care of the animals. They need you. So wake up now."

He woke up on the floor beside the pit. There was a strange stirring and fluttering among the birds. The squirrels were chattering also, and rustling sounds came from all the cages. He could hear the dogs barking in the pens in the yard.

The light still streamed in through the open door, but now it had become a flickering red cloud, like the sheet lightning seen in the distance on a sultry summer night. He saw a red light flickering on the ceiling above him, and turned to see it through the doorway into the office, dancing on the wall there. He smelled the wood burning and the smell of hot dirty oil.

He jumped to his feet. In the dull red light he saw Harry stretched out in the pit, one arm flung out, sleeping soundly. He ran to the door of the office. The whole corner near the outer door was in flames, and the barrel was burning like a stove. Slumped over the desk were Johnny Burton, face down on the bare wood, and the marshal, sleeping on one arm, the other stretched out straight with its bandaged hand propped up on the telephone.

"Wake up!" Jody yelled, but neither of them stirred. He ran to the marshal and shook him hard. "Marshal, get up!" The marshal only groaned.

Jody picked up his broom from the corner and beat the marshal around the head and across his bandaged hand with it. At the first blow the marshal yelled in pain, at the second he swung at Jody and knocked him sprawling.

"What the hell," the marshal shouted, and jumped up at the desk.

"We've got to get out!" Jody yelled at him. "Everything's on fire!"

He scrambled up and started shaking Johnny by the shoulders, hard, until Johnny stumbled clumsily to his feet. The marshal stood as if in a daze.

"I've got to have that key!" Jody shouted.

"What?" the marshal said.

"Key, the key to the handcuffs, I've got to have that key so I can get Harry out of the pit!"

The marshal stood stock-still, staring at him in the red light.

"Oh God," he said.

"Where is the key?" Jody shouted.

"At home, in my other clothes."

They looked at one another unmoving. A plank fell in flames from the wall near the door.

"What in hell's going on?" asked Johnny, his voice thick with sleep.

"Come on!" Jody said, grabbing and tugging at them, "Come on! Let's try to pull Harry loose."

He half-pushed, half-dragged them out of the office into the garage. Harry was still asleep. Johnny stopped in the doorway and looked back at the fire. He was awake now and sober.

"My Lord," he said, "the whole place is gonna burn like kindling."

"Lend a hand," the marshal said, scrambling down into the pit.

Harry stirred and sat up. "What is—"

"It's a fire," the marshal said, "and I don't have the key to get you out."

Harry struggled to his knees. He pulled the handcuff taut, trying it out, and the chain to which he was cuffed stretched out tight in every direction. The birds and small animals in their cages fluttered and chattered.

"Everybody grab that chain somewheres," the marshal said, "and all pull together."

He took the chain in both hands. Jody and Johnny grabbed hold too, and they all heaved. The rows of cages shook and swayed, but nothing gave way. The cages looked flimsy, but tucked in their pit like stones in an arch, their frames reinforced one another. The harder the men pulled the more firmly the cages resisted.

"No use," the marshal said, after half a dozen tries. "We got to have an ax or a wrecking bar or something."

Harry looked at them wildly. "They ain't much time."

"I know," the marshal said. "Johnny, run see if you can raise Art. Maybe he's got something like that. I'll try the judge's place."

Johnny took off in a run through the back door.

"I'm sorry, Harry," the marshal said. "We'll hurry all we can." He ducked his eyes and ran past Jody, who was still tugging at the chain.

He and Harry looked at one another. Jody dropped the chain and sat down on the floor with him.

"I ain't gonna make it," Harry said. "This is it fer me." He shuddered a little. "Wish I had Bill's razor or a gun or something.

Lord, I don't want to burn in this place." He looked around him at the animals and birds. "It's gettin' hot." He gave another frantic heave at the chain, then dropped it and looked back at Jody.

"Get out of here," he said. "Take that box with the money and give it to Rose. Tell her all abut it."

Jody didn't move.

"Get out, damn it! It's all over."

"The truck!" Jody yelled. He had a sudden vision of Harry's truck lifting Bill's coffin out of the grave. "Give me the truck keys! We'll pull you out."

Harry raised his head and his eyes lit up. He understood at once. "My right front pocket," he said. "I can't reach them."

Frantically Jody dug them out. He raced out the door with the keys to where the truck sat. He clambered in, his hands trembling badly, fumbling with the keys.

Hey, get hold of yourself, his mind said. He forced himself to stop shaking. He tried a key in the ignition switch, then the other. He had never driven anything, but he had watched. He pushed in the clutch, got the motor started on the second try, and put the gear where he knew reverse should be. He let it out too fast, and killed the motor. Next time he gunned the motor while he let out the clutch, and the truck bucked and roared but moved. Awkwardly, in a wide circle, he steered it crazily back toward the door. He forgot to brake, and the tailgate smacked into the door with a jolt and a sound of splintering, and the motor killed itself.

He ran around and climbed into the truck bed and kicked away what he could of the door frame. The opposite wall between garage and office was beginning to burn now. He tossed the tow chain into the garage and scrambled through after it. He threw a loop around the truck frame as he had seen Harry do at the grave.

"You got to tear away some of that wall," Harry yelled. Already the noise of the fire made it hard to hear what he said.

Jody understood. He wrapped the chain around the frame on one side of the door, then took the hook over to the next stud, kicked loose a wallboard, and hooked the chain around the stud. Then he jumped back in the truck, started it again, found low gear, and lurched forward. He gunned the motor and a great piece of the wall came out in splinters. He didn't wait to clear the debris, but backed up again, crawled under the truck among the splintered boards, and retrieved the chain. He dragged the free end to Harry.

"This might work," Harry said. He gathered up the chains to which he was cuffed and forced them into the hook.

"It's all gonna come out in a tangle," Jody said. "You're gonna get cut up pretty bad." He was shouting now to make himself heard over the crackle and roar.

"Never mind that," Harry said. "Just go right on. I'll duck and fend as I can. It's better than burning."

"Watch the steps when you come out, and the wall. I'll try to go steady and not too fast." He ran to the truck.

"Jody!" Harry yelled. Jody stopped and turned. "Take the money!"

Jody grabbed the box and tucked it under an arm. He scrambled out, climbed in the cab, threw the box under the seat, and started the motor. He found a forward gear, after some grinding, and raced the motor while he eased up on the clutch. The motor clattered as he moved forward slowly. He felt the chain go taut and kept tugging steadily until the load began to give, slowly, ever so slowly.

He looked back and saw the cages buckling, twisting, breaking, wire tangling, boards splintering. Harry was in the middle of it, trying to keep his feet, pushing the debris away from him, bouncing his way through the hole where the door was. The chains behind him were dragging the entrails of the pit along the rocky ground, and the animals penned with him were scurrying to their freedom. Behind them the fire raged like a maddened beast deprived of prey.

He kept dragging everything until they were out into the street, well away from the burning building. Then he killed the motor and hurried around to where Harry sat on the ground.

"Wow. What a ride," Harry said.

He was badly scratched and cut. A big splinter of a clapboard had pushed through his shirt and bloodied his side. It still hung there and dragged on the ground beside him. One arm hung twisted at a strange angle.

"I gotta get you some help," Jody said.

"Never mind right now," Harry said. "That'll wait. I'm all right. See if you can get some of those animals out of there."

He left Harry and ran back to the garage. All along the north wall, the cages were full of frantic creatures, while the south wall was a sheet of flame. He raced along the wall of cages, pulling them open, while the fluttering, squawking, scurrying birds and small animals flopped and scrambled to their freedom. He had barely opened the last cages when the east wall exploded in flame.

He ran from the building into the fenced lot behind, where the dog pens and the outbuildings were surrounded by dry blue–stem grass nearly waist–high. The whole building was on fire now, throwing red smoke into the sky and lurid red splotches and shadows all around him. The heat was blistering, searing. He ran from pen to pen, throwing them open, in the midst of barking and yowling. The dogs and cats shot from their cages, leaped the fence or wriggled through, and were gone.

Some of them were having trouble. A pup seemed confused, couldn't get over the fence or through it. Jody called him, but he wouldn't come. Jody chased him down, caught him, and handed him over the fence.

Then Rupe. Rupe shot from his cage when Jody turned him loose and made a hobbling run at the fence. Because he couldn't run as fast, he couldn't jump as well with only three legs, and he couldn't get over. He made run after run at it, but fell back every time.

Jody tried to coax Rupe back toward the gate to the pen, but that way was the burning building, and the grass fire moving steadily down the lot. Then Jody tried to catch him, but he snarled, showed his teeth, and scrambled away.

"Come on, Boy. I won't hurt you." But Rupe wasn't going to trust him at all. The grass fire came on, and Rupe and Jody and a distracted raccoon were soon to be pushed up against the fence.

Jody clambered over the hog–wire fence and began to tear at the wire with his hands and kick it with his feet. By sheer force, he managed to dislodge some staples. He yanked and heaved on the wire until he stretched it up from the ground a few inches. The raccoon wriggled under and was gone. Rupe put his head under the wire, but was too big to get through.

Jody let the wire go down on Rupe's neck and climbed back over inside the pen. Rupe was snarling now. Jody took him around the middle, though the dog's claws tore at him wildly, and tugged his head back from under the fence. Rupe thrashed and kicked, but Jody hung on. When his head came free, Rupe reached around and snapped with his teeth at Jody's arms and hands and face. Jody wouldn't let him go. By mere clumsy force he heaved the thrashing, squirming body over the fence and dropped him on the other side.

Then he scrambled back over himself and began running to get out of the way of the grass fire. It came on in a wide arc, and the last few yards he had to run through the wall of fire and then over the glowing smoldering clumps of grass. He knew his clothes were afire. At last he was out in the open. He threw himself on the ground and rolled over and over, then sat up and batted at his smoldering trouser legs until the flames were out.

Suddenly he felt very tired. He got up slowly and walked back to the truck where Harry sat. Harry looked up at him from a face drawn with pain.

"Help me a little here," he said.

With his good arm, he had dragged the chain and the tangle of wire and splintered frames toward him. He was reaching for one twisted cage, just out of his reach. There was something in it, a ball of gray fur, hand-like feet with claws gripping the chicken wire firmly, a long leathery tail. The cage itself was a grotesquely twisted mesh with some splinters hanging uselessly by their staples.

Jody lifted the tangled mass from the ground and brought the possum to Harry, then sat down beside him and began untwisting the mesh. Little by little he stretched the wire away, until finally he could pull it apart and disentangle the possum. The body was limp in his hands.

"He's dead, Harry."

"Maybe not," Harry said. "You know how they play dead."

Jody's hands explored the body. "No," he said, "his back's broke and his rib cage is crushed."

He laid the possum on Harry's knee. Harry gathered the possum up in his good hand and cradled him in his arm. His fingers stroked the gray fur.

They sat silently together and watched the Animal Store burn. The grass fire made a red crooked line in the darkness, running down the field behind the store where it would burn itself out at the creek. People were beginning to come now. Johnny came running back, along with Art in his trousers, carrying a wrecking bar and a bolt cutter. Art cut the chain and then the handcuffs from Harry's broken arm. Art's wife came hurrying behind him in her housecoat. Sally was in her nightgown. The marshal and the judge came trotting up a minute later, and on their heels came Doc lugging his kit.

Doc looked at them both. "I don't know where to start."

"Harry's got a broken arm and a gash in his side," Jody said. "I ain't hurt."

Doc looked at him strangely, but he turned to Harry. "Let's see how bad that gash is." He dropped down on his knees beside Harry.

Harry handed the possum to the marshal. The marshal took it in his hands and looked at it numbly.

Doc had opened his kit and was cutting and tearing Harry's shirt away from the wound. "It could be worse. Somebody break up some of these boards for splints. We'll have to get him to Ashton to the hospital."

Jody reached for a splintered board.

"Not you," Doc said. "You sit real still until I can see how bad those burns are. Better yet, lie down and be quiet."

"Burns?" Jody said. Almost as if on signal he began to feel the pain. He looked down at his arm and saw the skin hanging in a huge blister.

More people came running. Sally stood looking at him like an apparition in white.

Doc turned quickly to Jody and began cutting away clothing from his legs. "I need cold water, and towels, lots of them."

Suddenly Jody started going to sleep. All the people were simply standing there, watching him and Harry, in the red glow. He saw the Animal Store as a mere glowing skeleton. Then the ridge pole and rafters slowly sagged and dropped inward. As he closed his eyes he could see it in his mind, sagging down, down, until the glowing timbers broke and tumbled in charcoal into the open pit.

Chapter Sixteen

Then came long, long days full of pain and discomfort, all through the blistering August. Most of the time those days he lay on a cot in the shade of the huge red oak in his front yard at home. It was the coolest place they could find for him, and what breeze was stirring always played there. He slept a lot, especially at first. While he was awake he would lie listening to the locusts make their monotonous music, and the cardinals and jays, or in the evening turtle–doves and then whippoorwill. Hummingbirds came to visit the mimosa trees, and the squirrels ran through the woods at the edge of the clearing, leaping gracefully from tree to tree and never coming to earth. He read for long hours from the few books his scanty library provided. Except for the pain and the tiredness that seemed to intend never to go away, it was not a bad time. It was hard to explain why, but it was a time of rest and peace.

Doc came out from town to check on him, daily at first, then less often. Usually somebody from town came with him simply to see Jody and talk with him a while. There were some of the boys from town his own age that he had never got to know very well. They rode along with Doc to see the wounds dressed and talk with Jody and get him to tell about the fire again and again.

Others came too. Art and his wife brought Mrs. Gamble out one Sunday afternoon. Sally came with them, and after the grown–ups went off together to the house, Sally stayed with Jody and talked about how he was going to miss the first of school. She said that maybe she could get her folks to bring her out on Sunday afternoons so she could help him keep up in his studies. She smiled, and once she brushed her arm against him thoughtlessly and made him take in his breath sharply. When she was leaving, she reached over and squeezed his hand and left him with a smile on his face that lasted the rest of the day.

Mostly it was his own family who cheered him up and cared for him. Little Tommy had made it his special task to bring him cool, fresh water. About every hour he brought fresh water, almost before what he had last brought could get warm. He sat by Jody hour after hour, even when they had nothing more to say. His mother would come to change the dressings, and would sit to talk to him or read to him. Often the worst nights he would wake himself moaning in his sleep with pain and restlessness, and there she would be sitting up beside him. On the weekends when his dad came home, it almost seemed he couldn't be away from Jody. He told Jody over and over how proud he was of him, how brave his son must be, how good, how much he loved him. Jody tried to protest. It was strange, it made him uneasy for his father to praise him and say such things.

"I don't feel brave," he said one day, "and it don't feel right fer you to say it."

"Let be, Son," Josh said. "You might even be right fer all we know—only the Lord Almighty knows what we're really made of. You got to understand me. I need to tell you how I feel. I think over and over, what if you'd died in that fire, and I'd never told you these things. They has got to be said. So let your old dad have his say, and believe me that I mean it all."

Jody was quiet then, lying on his cot, his hand resting on his dad's arm where he sat on the ground alongside. After a while he said, "Then if you feel that way, maybe you'd better know something more, and maybe you can help me know what to do."

So he told Josh the whole story of the night he had looked at Bill and Rose, every detail of it, just as he had told the sheriff. He told all about his interview with the sheriff the next day, and about the shoe and the marshal's continuing suspicion of Harry. His dad listened carefully, reassuring him in the hard places by taking his hand gently, and it all came out without so much effort after all. Afterward Josh was quiet for a long time.

"Did I do a great wrong?" Jody asked, at last.

"Yes, Son, you was wrong. When a person shares a shame with you, like you have just done with me, it's a great privilege he's done you, 'cause you've been trusted to understand and forgive and help bear. But when you trespass on a person's shame, you've taken away something she never agreed to share."

Jody closed his eyes. "So I wronged Bill Becker and Rose. Bill is dead, and if I tell Rose it'll hurt her."

Josh patted his arm. "Son, Son," he said, "try to remember you ain't Jesus Christ or God Almighty. You done wrong. Well, we all do. And something else, in case you don't know. You'll likely do wrong again. That's why we just got to forgive one another. They ain't nothing else we can do."

"How can Bill Becker forgive me?"

Josh smiled. "You see it ain't all that cut and dried. It would of been nice to hear Bill say so, but just having someone say 'I forgive you' may not make that much difference anyway. People are able to forgive if they're able to ask to be forgave. It's the same thing. Either way, it's a state o' heart. Bill asked fer your forgiveness, and the moment he really wanted it, he was a–forgiving everything wrong ever done him, whether he knowed it or not."

Something broke loose in Jody's chest. "Then maybe the Lord forgave Bill fer his suicide."

"You see," Josh said, "we don't know. All we really know is, the Lord knows a lot more about forgiveness than you or me. He's done a lot more of it, and he does a better job of it."

Jody turned that over in his mind. At last he said, "I guess then I'll just have to let be. What should I do about Rose?"

"I can't tell you, Son," Josh said. "If you want forgiveness, you gotta ask. The rest of that problem is whether Rose can forgive you. That's where the risk comes in. If there weren't no risk, of course, there wouldn't be no forgiveness anyway. It wouldn't mean nothing. And it ain't just a risk fer you. It's a risk fer her too, like I been saying."

He thought and thought about that, day after day. Rose had been out to see him in Harry's truck three times. Harry was still too sore from his wound to move around much. Soon they would come out together, and sit and talk and laugh about what had happened. Should he risk the loss of that? Should he let them really know, when they thought and everybody thought he had been a hero or something? Should he hurt and humiliate Rose by telling her what he knew about her, and could he tell her without telling Harry? And how could he tell Harry about Rose?

While he was still turning it over and over, Rose came out one day. The old truck clattered up through the woods to the clearing where the house stood, jouncing over the outcroppings of sandrock at the edge of the yard. Rose parked in the shade of his big oak and climbed out. She always said Hello at first and went to talk awhile with Mrs. Carpenter, and then came back to talk an hour with Jody, bringing news about the folks in town and long detailed accounts of how Harry was healing and what Doc said about his wound, and on and on. Most of the news Jody already knew, and Rose knew he knew. The point rather was being there, the talking, the seeing one another, and visiting for Harry by proxy. Jody understood that, so he always patiently heard her stories over again.

"Harry says he's coming out next time, if Doc says he can," Rose said. "He said to tell you he's making you something. I ain't supposed to tell what, but he's carving something out of that board that stuck him in the side, fer a keepsake. The left arm's getting strong enough to hold it still now whilst he whittles."

"Rose," Jody said, "there's something I got to tell you."

Rose stopped and looked at him strangely.

"This ain't gonna be easy," Jody said. "When I'm through, you may not ever want to talk to me again."

Rose's face grew soft. "I don't rightly see how that could be. There ain't nothing you can tell me that can make me feel like that."

Jody swallowed hard. "It could be, though. Just listen, Rose."

He took a moment to gather his courage, then plunged in.

"You remember the marshal asking you about someone who had been prowling round your house. Well, that was me. I was there looking in when you and Bill come home that last night, and I seen everything."

Rose sat motionless, expressionless. After a long time, she spoke. "You seen everything?"

"I seen it all, Rose, and I hope you can forgive me. I'm so sorry."

"So you know," Rose said. Tears welled in her eyes and her shoulders slumped. "All my secrets, all about Bill and me, all about—all about the puppy."

She blushed crimson. Through the sparse blond hair, Jody could see even her scalp was red.

"You had no right to know!" she said suddenly, quietly but with force.

"That's so."

"You was just sneaking round, like a dirty little pervert."

"No," Jody said, his head bent over. Then he raised his eyes and looked at her. "Yes."

Rose looked at him hard for a long, long time. At last she wiped her eyes and took a long breath. "Oh Jody, Jody," she said. She looked off into the distance. "Well, it takes one to know one. I ain't in much position to call anyone nasty."

She pulled a big handkerchief out of her bosom and mopped her eyes. "All them years with Bill. I loved him so much, but it was just one long frustration. Do you know, I tried to seduce a kid once. He just laughed at me and called me an old fat bitch. I cried and cried, and finally I said to myself, 'serves you right, you old fat bitch.' And so I got along as best I could. It just wouldn't go away. So I says, finally, I'll just tough it out. Pretty soon I'll get old and then it won't be so rough, and then likely I'll die."

She took a long, long look into Jody's eyes. Then she gave a big, horsy laugh. "Well, so what, huh? So life's hard. What else is new?" She gave Jody a slap on the shoulder, pretty hard, and then laid her hand gently on the shoulder she had hit.

"You been carrying that around and feeling bad ever since Bill died, right? Well, let it go, little friend. It's all right. You're still the man that helped me dig two graves by lantern light, and buried my old man fer me, and pulled my Harry out of the fire."

Jody laid his hand on her hand. "Thanks, Rose."

"One more thing," Rose said. "I want you to know that I told Harry all about it."

Jody drew a sharp breath. "That's amazing."

Rose laughed. "Yeah, I kind of amazed myself. Harry, well, you know Harry by now. He took it all in stride. I guess if Harry can handle it, I can." She laughed again. Then she took her hand from Jody's shoulder and straightened her hair. She smiled and her face fell into repose. "I'm gonna marry Harry, Jody. We ain't told anyone yet, but Harry wants you to be best man. Then we're gonna see whether life can't be better than it's ever been fer both of us."

Jody said. "I owe Harry something too. Hadn't been fer me, the marshal might not of made such a big deal of his investigation. Maybe if it hadn't been fer me, Harry wouldn't a been in that pit in the first place."

Rose laughed. "And if my old pa hadn't been a drunk, I'd a never left Arkansaw. No point in playing what–if games, Jody. What's done is done, and you go on from where you're at."

The following day the judge came out in his DeSoto. The car scraped its bottom on the sandrock as he pulled in the yard. The judge got out, got on his knees, and looked underneath the car.

Jody laid down his book and sat up. "Did you break anything?"

"No damage done," the judge said and clambered heavily to his feet.

"This road's made fer wagons and pickups and Model A's."

"I'll have to watch that rock next time," the judge said. He came over and sat on the foot of Jody's cot. "How are you feeling?"

"I'm doing fine," Jody said. "Doc says I may be a few weeks late entering school this year, but that's okay. I got some help," he grinned and blushed, "and I'll catch up easy."

The judge looked over the books Jody had by the cot. Besides the Bible, there was *Pilgrim's Progress*, an American history, an old battered volume called *British Poets of the Nineteenth Century*, and an old book with the covers off called *A Serious Call to a Devout and Holy Life* by someone called William Law. The history and poetry books were old textbooks his mother had got when her folks died. The book without a cover was one Josh had found in a corner of the building he was painting.

"You read a lot, don't you?" the judge said.

"I read the same things over and over," Jody said. "They ain't much around here to read."

"Tell you what," the judge said, "I've got some books I'll never read again, just taking up room in my house. If you don't mind, I'll bring them out and leave them with you. When you're through with them, you can keep what you want and give the rest to the school."

"I'd like that."

"How long until you're out of school?"

"Three years, if I don't have to stop and work."

The judge took out a fresh cigar and lit it. He studied Jody's face carefully. "Then what? Are you going to college?"

"Oh, well, I don't know," said Jody, looking away. He thumbed the edge of the *British Poets* wistfully.

The judge took a long puff on his cigar and blew the smoke out in a cloud. "I shouldn't smoke these things anymore, old as I am.

Doc tells me whenever he sees me light one how bad they are for me. I'm getting to be an old relic." He took another puff. "But let's suppose I'm still around in three years. I want you to come have a talk with me about how important it is for you to go to college."

He picked up *A Serious Call*, opened it at random, and read a few lines while the smoke drifted around his thin gray hair. "What a pity."

"What's a pity?" Jody asked.

"For things like this to have been known and written and people not to know about them." He closed the old book and laid it gently on the Bible. "What a colossal waste."

He stood and looked out over the landscape where it fell away from the crown of the clearing, mile after mile, his hands folded behind him, holding the cigar. "If I'm not here in three years," he said, not turning around, "I want you to go see Lonnie Yates. He'll have a letter for you, a very important letter." He turned around and looked at Jody.

"Sure, Judge," Jody said, "but why three years? Why not now?"

The judge smiled. "As Harry said once, it would take away."

In late August the marshal came to see him. He hadn't seen the marshal since the fire, and he was a bit surprised to see the old truck come grinding up the hill. It was the marshal, all right. On the back of the truck were some wire cages. He's been out gathering up animals, Jody thought.

"I just wanted to say hello," the marshal said. "Looks like you're healing okay."

"Sure," Jody said.

"My hand's healed up fine," the marshal said, flexing it freely.

"I see you got a new badge."

"Yep," the marshal said, fingering the star on his shirt pocket. "It's a different kind of badge. Sheriff Yates has made me a deputy. We got this new system now, where all the town marshals is Yates's deputies. We meet twice a month, and Lonnie comes by or calls ever so often."

"Are you still collecting animals?"

"Well, yes, but not like the old days. I ain't gonna try to run a store. It's too much trouble anyway. All I do now is pick up cats and dogs that's running round town without a collar. If the owners don't pen them up and give them rabies shots, they has to pay a fine."

He bit off a chew from his plug of tobacco and then took a bill out of his pocket. "What with the fire and all, I never did pay you that last week's wages." He handed Jody the five dollars. "I wanted to do that. You was real good help."

"Thanks," Jody said, taking the bill.

"I been doing the garbage run all by myself again," he went on. "I plumb forgot how much more work it was, afore you come. I just take everything and bury it all together now, though. I don't try to sort nothing no more. I put it all in the same hole, down in the old lot where the store was."

"That's easier," Jody said.

"You know, it is," the marshal said, "and cleaner too." He got up from where he had squatted down. "I got to be going. I just wanted to come and pay you." He walked over to the back of the truck, then turned dramatically. "Well, really, they was one other thing. I wanted to say I was real glad you got Harry out of that pit, and—well, I wanted to say I was real glad."

"Sure," Jody said.

"Matter of fact, I brought you something. Don't rightly know what else to do with this, but thought maybe you'd like to have it."

He hefted one of the large cages down from the truck. "I found this out at the edge of town." He lifted the gate of the cage and kicked the back of it lightly.

Out of the cage came a thin chow dog with one missing forepaw.

"Rupe!"

The dog came slowly, with that hopping limp of his, up to Jody's cot. He licked at the boy's hand and waved his tail.

The marshal spat, hefted the empty cage back in his truck, and slammed the tailgate. He stood looking at the dog and boy caressing one another.

"See you take good care of that dog," he said. "That dog's a champion."

And for the first time, Jody saw the marshal's long, leathery face break into a smile.

THE END